ALSO BY ALESSANDRA VU

Bargain with the Devil series
Paranormal Fantasy Romance
Bargain with the Devil – September 2024
Becoming the Devil – September 2025
Book III – September 2026

Standalone
Dark Romantasy
The Wolf and His Prey – June 2025

The Wolf and His Prey

A Novella By
Alessandra Vu

THE WOLF AND HIS PREY

First edition. June 30th, 2025

Copyright © 2025 Alessandra Vu.

Book Cover Design: Juniper Hartman at The Red Fox Creative – modifications made by Alessandra Vu in GIMP

ISBN: 979-8-9906682-3-2

Written by Alessandra Vu.

dedication

to my postpartum self:
it was a struggle.
but you did it.

Author's Note

Regarding Content

This is a **dark** fantasy romance. There is racism, sexism, wealth disparity, graphic violence, murder, stalking, and attempted murder on the page. There is an unhealthy depiction of obsession by one of the characters towards another character. There are explicit sexual scenes.

I do not condone nor promote their behavior. I write characters that match and fit each other well and sometimes that means they are a toxic match instead of a healthy representation of a romantic relationship.

In simple, blunt words: my depiction is not my endorsement.

For those who wish to continue on with reading, I hope you enjoy.

Thank you.

Chapter One

Gryphon

- five years ago -

Blood STAINS THE pristine white snow and I'm reminded of the cherry flavored winter delicacy my mother so loved. She'd spend the summers collecting every wild cherry she could find, mashing them down and running them through a cheesecloth till only liquid remained. No matter how bitter and cold the winters ran, she'd drizzle that delectable cherry syrup she worked so hard for atop the small mountain of snow she collected in a bowl. The years her body became too brittle and frail, I carried on that tradition until her last dying breath came into existence two winters ago.

Air violently swirls around me while the snow offers meek shelter from the harsh conditions. A deep ache in my wrist throbs and I glare down at the snare slicing its way through my joint. As much as I loathe to admit it, whoever designed such an apparatus has my utmost respect. Try as I might, the more I move to free myself, the harder the trap clamps down.

Steam rises from the warm blood melting through snow, a rather bleak reminder of how cold it's become. Should I remain outside overnight, I might not return home with as many fingers and toes as I left with. How unfortunate for me, then, that it is a *hand* caught in the snare and not a foot. Without the strength of two arms to pry the device open, I fail to see how I will escape.

Eventually, the owner of the trap will come along to reset the snare, but there is no way for me to know how many hours, days, or weeks that will be. I need to procure a solution of my own, one that requires a hand instead of two.

I might dig the stake out of the ground and carry the trap with me into town, but that would require shifting forms. A naked body won't do well in weather such as this. The town, whose name escapes me, is too far from where I'm stranded and the black, thick fur that covers me head to toe shields me from the elements in ways the piled snow cannot. Still, it may be the only plan I have.

Seconds drag into minutes as no other ideas come to mind and finally, I relent. Crunching of bones are muffled by strong winds as fur fades away to pale skin, pointed ears shrink to rounded, and an intimidating maw shifts to a simple nose and mouth. Bone chilling air lashes against my bare back the moment I shift, sending a brutal and cold tremble wracking through me. As soon as I'm able to, the fingers of my free hand dig through the snow to the frozen ground where the stake resides. It is a wonder the owner of the trap was able to nail it so firmly and so late in the season, but that is admiration due for another day.

Numb fingers curl around the chain links secured at the top of the stake and I yank as hard as my gifted body allows. There is no give. The stake is frozen deep into the ground. White puffs of air huff out my mouth as I yank again and I realize, belatedly, my wet fingers have adhered to the bitingly cold metal.

"Fuck," I growl to the emptiness of the forest.

Two hands now trapped and naked as the day I was born.

I shift back, sighing into the warmth of the fur coat as it consumes me and tug my hand free of the stake. Bits of flesh remain stuck to the metal, but I'm far too numb to feel any of it. An angry huff exhales from me as I scowl at the snare. What the devil is it doing out here in the forest anyway? I've seen no houses nearby that might inform me who the trap belongs to. There is no livestock it is protecting. It is a trap far too big for hare and smaller game. It is meant for bears and, unfortunately, *me*.

Click.

My head snaps east towards the sound and I stare down the barrel of a rifle. Behind it stands a woman, wisps of fiery orange hair fluttering around her eyes despite the hat upon her head. She's bundled in brown wool clothes, but her face is bare to the elements. Freckled skin, reddened by the harsh wind, and pale blue eyes squint at me from twenty paces back. Determination lines her face, but she dares not approach the massive beast.

She encompasses the beauty of my dreams, the yearning deep within my heart. I have never gazed upon another so exquisite, so blasé to the danger that stands before them. She holds no false sense of protection behind that gun yet does not cower at my presence.

She is beautiful.

My tongue swipes out, licking the length of my jaw as my eyes sweep down her body. Even bundled as she is, I can imagine the silhouetted frame hidden from me, how pale and littered with freckles it must be. Fire ignites within my veins as I shift forward towards her, unable to stay away. Her fingers tighten around the gun, pale blue eyes darting to the snare around my wrist. Her carmine lips pull downward, sending a thrill racing through my body.

Mine. All *mine.*

I edge forward once more, wrist flaring to life as the metal teeth dig further into my joint, but I cannot find it in me to care. She's enraptured me. I *must* have her.

She tilts her head backwards, peering down the length of her nose at me.

"How did you get to become so big, wolf?" she asks with an even and melodious voice as her eyes study my size. "It is unnatural."

Indeed, it is. Nothing good ever comes of a man who is beast and a beast who is man.

"I should kill you," she says as she adjusts the butt of the rifle resting against her shoulder. "Your fur alone will fetch a hefty price."

If she deems me worthy of death, I will not refute it. For she is mine and I am hers and that is how it is to be.

She regards me for a few silent moments, tilting her head to the side as unease surfaces on her hardened face.

"Your eyes..." she trails off as the barrel of the gun dips down towards the snow. "They seem almost human."

My head tilts sideways as I wonder what it is she sees. None has ever seen me for more than a terrifying beast. Shrieks and screams and cries are my welcome wherever I step foot. No one is able to see past the lethal predator that walks amongst them. No one... but *her.*

"You don't seem to be suffering," she states as she glances quickly at my body. "If I offer help, will you harm me?"

And what of the money?

Silence lingers in the air as I wait for an answer that will never come. Her finger holding the barrel taps against the surface as she debates her options. Kill me for money or risk a mauling in an attempt to free me?

She hesitates only for a moment before approaching, the mouth of the gun still pointed at me. I do not move, not wanting to startle my little rabbit. She never discards her weapon, only shifting it out of the way as she kneels in the snow. She is unbothered by the blood staining the ground and hesitantly reaches for the snare. Bare fingers edge their way into the empty space between metal teeth and my wrist and she tugs against the device.

I watch her as her eyebrows furrow, as her teeth bite down on her lip, and I cannot suppress the animalistic growl that overcomes me. She immediately retreats, gun raised as white puffs of air float around her face.

"Do not harm me or I will leave you here to die," she orders, voice trembling in fear.

How I yearn to hear it tremble with unbridled enthusiasm.

My head nods at her, the snout of my nose nudging beneath her forearm in quiet encouragement. She's as stiff as a board, eyes watching me for any sudden movements, but they never come. Calmly, I wait. Even as the cold air chills us to the bone and the gray sky darkens.

She attempts again, fingers straining against the contraption as she pulls against it. It takes her a couple of tries before there's enough space for me to slip my hand through. It does not slide out with ease, but nevertheless, I am free. She hastily darts back, anticipating an attack from me, her chest rising and falling as white puffs cloud her face. I do not move as I regard her.

Where has she come from?

What is she doing in the forest?

Is this *her* trap?

"Go on now," she urges with a wave of her hand. "You're free to go home."

Ah, yes, but what of my injured wrist?

Her gaze darts down to my injured joint as if she can hear the thoughts rumbling within my head.

"Does it hurt?"

Atrociously so.

Her pale blue eyes glance around the forest, wind whipping her fiery orange hair into her face. Not but a moment later, the wind rips the hat straight off her head, sending long locks of hair spiraling in the wind. Hints of rosemary taint the air whenever her hair gets too close and the urge to bury my nose deep within those tresses nearly overwhelms me.

Her hands quickly grab hold of the hair as best they can, spooling it into a mess at the nape of her neck. She glances at me again, slowly grabbing the gun before rising onto her feet.

"I'll come check on you tomorrow," she says as she takes a gradual step back. "But I hope not to see you."

Such cruel words, my little rabbit.

"You better be well enough and gone by the time I come back," she urges as she takes another step back. "Or I may just finish the job and sell your fur."

My lips pull back in a grin, razor sharp teeth on display as a huff of amusement escapes my mouth. Her eyebrows cinch together, that unease slipping its way back onto her face as I react a bit too humanly for the beast that I am.

If it is fur you want, then fur you take.

She offers me one last lingering stare before turning and heading back the way she came. She does not appear lost, her steps assured, as she disappears into the thick trees of the forest. My heart aches in my chest, desperation filling me to the bone as I rise up onto my good hand and feet.

Mine. All *mine.*

My gaze glances around, landing on the town lingering in the distance. If I am to make her mine, I must make the town mine. I will become irrefutable in her eyes. There will be nothing I could not do for her. She will be mine and mine alone, never straying from my hungry gaze.

I *will* have her, but first...

I will have the town.

Chapter Two

Elvira

- present day -

"HAVE YOU HEARD? The new duke is moving into the Lockwood Estate today. I hope we might catch a glimpse of him," Annalise giddily declares as she plops a sugar cube into her teacup.

She has perfectly situated herself by the window, granting any wandering soul a full view of her beauty. The overcast sky does little to highlight the honey tones within her blonde hair, but it matters not as she has expertly pinned her hair out of her face while the back half beautifully spirals down her spine.

Annalise carefully holds back the hanging sleeve of her sapphire blue surcoat, the intricate patterns of her white, long sleeve underdress on full display as she plops another sugar cube into her teacup. She is a vision of piousness and innocence.

"I hear he makes ten thousand rysar a year," Lydia replies in kind, lazily stirring her demitasse spoon. "His estate only requires three thousand a year to be adequately managed. That means seven thousand rysar *a year* for a wife to spoil herself with... I warn you two now, do not judge me for my desperate attempts at garnering his attention."

Lydia is practically merging with the curtain, though her crimson red surcoat does little to help her remain invisible. Naturally black coily hair has been intricately braided and slicked back into a high ponytail, ribbons expertly woven into the braids as they dangle down, ghosting against her collars in a delicate and feminine display.

Annalise clicks her tongue, a frown marring her pale face. "You would marry him to gain access to his rysar and not for love?"

"You would too if you understood the importance of money," Lydia quips, her rich, russet brown face doing little to hide her vexation at Annalise's question.

They're oil and water, these two, and I the cruet that forces them together.

"What if he's ghastly?" I inquire sincerely as I lift the teacup to my lips.

"It matters not what he looks like if he makes ten thousand rysar a year," Lydia answers matter of fact. "Love will not warm your house or put food on your table. Nor will beauty and charm. He clearly has the wit and connections if he makes ten thousand rysar a year and that is all that matters."

She cannot hide the bitterness seeping into her tone and I do not miss the way Annalise rolls her lips inward to bite back the words that desire to rush forth. Lydia's family was not always so far down the societal ladder, making the sting of her current situation that much harsher. Wealth once had and lost is always harder to live with than never having wealth to begin with.

"Well," I begin lightly, not wanting to touch upon her past, "if he is truly ghastly than I wish him old age as well so you won't have to endure his company for long."

It earns a hearty laugh from Lydia.

"*Widowed* Duchess of Kilnorn has an alluring ring to it," Lydia hums much to my amusement.

Annalise, however, does not appreciate our humor.

"If there is no spark of love between us, then I simply do not want it," she states defiantly, brown eyes focused on the amber colored tea within her cup.

"You, and only you, will be lying in the bed your regrets have made, Annalise," Lydia replies sharply, words laced with wisdom and pain. "Best be wise about the choices you make."

"I will not marry solely for money," she snaps rather unlike herself. "It may be of great importance to *you*, but I have not lost something to yearn after."

"Annalise," I chide her, my eyes darting between her and Lydia.

Tension coils around us tight as a python, both women glaring at one another in challenge. *Oil and water and I the cruet.*

My lips part to offer an olive branch between the two but the words die within my mouth as a bell chimes throughout the small café we sit in. The door opens, a cold gust of wind rushing in as soon as the opportunity presents itself. Heads careen towards the door, hopeful eyes anticipating the newly appointed His Grace Gryphon Pike, Duke of Kilnorn and close friend of similarly newly appointed King Silas Ambrose the Third. Yet it is not him, merely Mira rushing in to greet her friends five tables over from where my friends and I sit.

Annalise openly frowns as she turns her attention back to the table, adding a *third* sugar cube to her tea.

"And what of you, Elvira?" Lydia inquires.

I'm not entirely certain I know what she's asking and my face must give my internal thoughts away because she quickly clarifies.

"Annalise will marry for love, I for money. Where do you stand?"

My lips purse to the side of my face, my fingers strumming against the warm surface of my teacup. Nearly twenty—eight summers have passed since my birth and yet I am no closer to being married than I was when I came crying out of the womb.

"It's hard to say when none has shown a flicker of interest," I answer.

"That's not true," Annalise quickly disagrees. "Mr. Corvin's boy was quite smitten with you. It's a shame you never returned his affections."

"Forgive me," I amend dramatically, offering a slight quirk of my lips towards Lydia, a secret smile only she is privy to. "Bram Corvin did fancy me quite a bit, but, as he was of bed wetting age, I never did allow him a courtship."

Upon hearing the clarification, Lydia rolls her eyes before directing her attention to Annalise.

"Heavens, Annalise, a child does not count."

"Even if she were a child as well?"

"Hearts of children are fickle compared to the hearts and deep pockets of men."

Annalise scoffs as she lifts her teacup to her mouth. Lydia's eyes slide over to mine, her lips terse as she levels me with a very open look of exasperation. It's no secret they would not be acquaintances if it were not for me. Days such as these, I often wonder why I bother forcing them together. One might claim me a martyr, but I only wish they would get along. They are, after all, the only friends I have. I suppose that's why they entertain me so when they do not desire to be friends themselves.

My thoughts churn over Lydia's question. Love or money? Times are decent now for my family, but my mind and body will never let me forget the months I starved, desperate for even a single bite of bread. Or the winters that bit at my toes and fingers, threatening to turn them blue, then black, immobilizing them for the rest of my life.

Today we are able to buy the food and clothes we need, but we're always one bad month away from the tides turning. To marry for love would be a privilege I'm not sure I can afford. The decent choice would be marrying for money if given the chance. Yet the prospect of marriage, for me, seems unlikely no matter the suitors wealth or appearance.

"Elvira?" Lydia asks, snapping me out of my thoughts.

My gaze drifts up to her questioning dark brown eyes and a weak smile plays at my lips.

"I think spinster is the better option," I state, forcing a laugh from my mouth.

It's a strange thing to not necessarily *want* to marry yet the vitriolic knowledge knowing that I'll never be considered has me yearning and sorrowful.

"With ten thousand rysar a year at my disposal, you'll want for nothing," Lydia declares knowingly.

My vision blurs as heat floods my cheeks. Lydia breathes life into the word loyalty and I have never felt more undeserving of such a friendship than I have after meeting her. Her words may be sharp, her past bitter and painful, but her heart is strong, fierce, and ready to fight for those she holds dear.

"You are far too kind," I whisper, my hand tentatively reaching towards her across the table.

The corner of her mouth twitches as she rolls her eyes out towards the window.

"Spinster?" Annalise asks, bewildered and ignorantly unaware. "You truly aspire to be a spinster?"

A disbelieving laugh falls from my mouth as I blink away the unshed tears. "I hardly see the issue with it."

"Well… think of your parents! They already have a hard enough time affording food for the house with you there. If you continue to remain there instead of finding a household of your own to manage… I hardly think that's kind towards your parents."

"And yet it is *I* who has such harsh, blunt words," Lydia mumbles into her teacup.

"Annalise, that's quite a rude thing to say, isn't it?" I ask, a certain bite to my words. "Especially addressed to a friend."

Her habit of pretending to not understand what she says rears its head within an instance. "What did I say? I'm sorry if my words were misspoken, I never meant such an offense. I merely meant you are far too beautiful and kind to become a spinster. If you desire it so, you *will* be married. I know it."

"Out of my rather… morbid curiosity, who do you suppose would be an acceptable suitor for our dear friend Elvira?" Lydia asks.

Annalise pauses to think, eyebrows furrowing towards her nose as she lightly nibbles her lip.

"Perhaps it is best to approach Bram Corvin," she offers thoughtfully. "A flicker of interest may still remain. Fond memories of a child have great influence over men. Gadaric Beckford will never let me forget our shared kiss despite us only being five years of age."

"Bram Corvin?" Lydia asks in a dull voice.

"Bram Corvin?" I repeat, eyebrows shooting up towards my hairline.

"Yes," Annalise replies, eyes innocently snapping up to mine as she nods her head curtly. "You might be surprised by what he'll say."

Bram Corvin would not be a suitor I would wish upon *any* soul. His vices are far too strong and, if it were not for the kindness of his father who owns his own business, Bram Corvin would not have the wherewithal to hold down a job.

"Annalise, have you slightest idea what Bram Corvin does with his free time?" I ask because I cannot fathom how she would suggest such a suitor while knowing the truth.

Her head cocks to the side slightly. "I trust he uses it to—"

The door swings wildly open, slamming against the frame as the bell chimes to announce a visitor. Cold wind whips violently inside the small shop, bringing with it drizzles of rain splattering across the wooden floor and the patrons sitting too close to the entrance.

A looming figure stands in the doorway, shoulders too broad for the black jacket adorning him. The black wool hooded chaperone hides his face well, droplets of water darting down the front and back of it. The movements of his body are rigid and stiff as he raises a left hand to toss back the hood. Shaggy, curly black hair cascades around a rough face.

A crooked nose. A scar at the top of the right eyebrow all the way down to the jawline. Dark, thick stubble broken up by the long scar. Strong brow. Lips turned downward. A face riddled by hardship and brutality. Handsome would be too generous a term for him, yet I cannot remove my gaze from him. His presence *commands* attention.

Dark amber eyes scan the room, no friendliness to be found. Such expressive eyes, so full of disdain. Yet what strikes me most is the *animalistic* nature of his stare. Predatory. Seeking. No, not seeking. *Hunting.* For what?

His left hand dives into those thick curls, shaking the locks furiously as if they were soaked in water, yet no droplets fly free from his hair.

As his hand falls away from his head, the gold ring on his pinky finger catches the light. It's unmistakable. The ring belongs to none other than the Duke of Kilnorn.

Almost instantly, the room shifts. The men closest to the duke rise from their seats, shamelessly peacocking in an attempt to curry his favor. The previous duke had no shortage of favorites, rotating through them as frequently as the days of the week.

His Grace Gryphon Pike, however, seems rather annoyed at the attention. As if he desires nothing more than to shrivel up and disappear beneath a rather large and unforgiving boulder.

How peculiar.

I haven't met many dukes in my life, but the ones I have always appeared to enjoy the attention. Their pride swelled and grew with the intoxicating power. Not this duke, though.

Despite being surrounded by men and women alike, desperately garnering for his attention, His Grace continues his hunt about the room. Those dark, amber eyes meet mine and they flash wild as his jaw sets.

Time stops.

His entire body turns in my direction as his eyes narrow, ravenous intent washing over his face as he takes a step towards my table.

My breathing hitches as my heart thunders against my chest.

He shoves past the people, his long strides taking him across the room in record time. He's brutish in size, far too big and rough *everywhere*. But it is his eyes that terrify me.

Such emotion. Such intent. Desire, hunger, and desperation fill those dark golden irises until they're overflowing. I can practically hear the possessiveness of his stare as he stops before me.

I swallow thickly, my breathing clipped as my body recoils from him. The hairs along my neck rise up, my pulse a jack rabbit against my neck. He *terrifies* me. He *fascinates* me. He is far too unrefined to be a duke, but there is no mistaking the golden ring settled on his pinky finger. Perhaps King Silas is playing a cruel joke on His Grace. Perhaps His Grace is meant to fail pitifully for the amusement of the king. Whatever the reason, I am at a loss for words as His Grace comes to a full stop in front of my seated form.

"Your name," he demands, his voice low and gruff.

His left hand reaches out towards me, not for me to take, but to clarify it is I he is speaking to. Callouses line his hand. *Not* the hand of a duke. The hand of a working man who toils away the day shaping shoes, bending metal, or sowing the land.

My eyes snap up to his, confusion swirling within the pit of my stomach.

"Elvira, Your Grace," I answer him.

"Elvira," he repeats my name as though he's speaking a foreign language, the syllables tight in his mouth.

"Elvira Noire," I clarify, acutely aware that the entire café listens to our every word.

"Annalise Augustine, Your Grace," Annalise chimes in, leaning towards me to draw his attention.

It does not work. He holds my gaze firmly as he drinks in my appearance. I feel spread out before him as if hooked and hung for his greedy hunter hands to skin me for his amusement.

"I hope you're settling in well," Annalise continues, her chair scraping against the wooden floor as her knees brush mine. "Kilnorn is quite beautiful this time of year. The leaves are surely due to change any day now. If it pleases you, it would be lovely to take a walk along the pond when the rain lets up."

He blinks, eyes darting down to my hands in my lap before meeting my stare again.

"It would bring me joy," he bites out, the words practically suffocating him as he holds my gaze, "to take a walk along the pond when the rain lets up, Elvira Noire."

"It would appear His Grace has little interest in either of us," Lydia speaks, directing her words towards Annalise.

There's no bitter resentment or frustration in her voice, but I do not miss the undertone of caution. There is something decidedly worrisome about the duke that I can neither put into words nor thoughts. Only a feeling. I take solace in Lydia's shared concern.

"She might feel better inclined to agree *after* Your Grace hosts a ball," Lydia offers. "You might share a dance or two, exchange pleasantries with one another before exploring a more intimate setting such as a walk along the pond."

"Yes," I eagerly agree, ever grateful for Lydia's wits. "A ball would be lovely, Your Grace. Might you be hosting one soon?"

His jaw clenches tight, eyes hardening as he glares at Lydia. If she feels threatened by it, she does not let on.

"I admit a ball is rather... out of my scope of talents," he declares unabashed.

"With ten thousand rysar a year, one would think you would have the funds to hire someone to help with that, no?" Lydia asks.

A low growl reverberates within his chest so softly I nearly miss it. I've never known a man to growl. Such an odd, yet enticing sound.

A huff of indignation expels from him as he glances back at me. "A ball would please you?"

"It has been quite some time since I've had the pleasure of attending a ball," I answer. "I would be more than happy to attend your ball."

"And you would save me a dance?" My lips part to answer, but he interjects quickly, his question rushing out as if it were all one word. "The first and last dance of the night?"

My lips press inward as I bury the smile begging to surface. Perhaps there isn't anything threatening about him but rather that he is *awkward*. The callouses on his hands and the scars on his body speak so clearly that the role of duke was never meant to be his, yet here he stands as the Duke of Kilnorn. It must be so very foreign to him.

The least I can offer him is my kindness.

"Yes, Your Grace," I answer, unable to keep the quirk of my lips down. "I will gladly save the first and last dance for you. It is your ball, after all."

He huffs out a breath of acceptance. "A ball it is, then."

"If it intrigues His Grace, might I offer my services for planning the ball?" Lydia asks.

His gaze shifts to hers, a frown pulling at his lips but he relents with one swift, curt nod. "State your price and I'll have a contract drawn up."

"One hundred rysar."

My head snaps to her in utter shock. One hundred rysar would feed my family for an entire year. How could she be so bold to ask such a high price?

Yet the duke is unphased as he nods his head.

"You will get fifty now and fifty after the ball," he says simply. "Stop by the estate to sign the contract at your earliest convenience."

"Of course, Your Grace."

Amber eyes slide to mine as he tilts his head downward. "Enjoy the rest of your day, Miss Noire."

"You as well, Your Grace," I reply in kind.

He wordlessly slides his hooded chaperone atop his head before turning and exiting the café quite abruptly. Silence ensues for only a few moments before the room bursts into gossip.

Lydia raises her teacup to her mouth, dark brown eyes scanning the room. A grimness settles over her features as her gaze shifts to me.

"You better arm yourself, Elvira Noire," she hums into her teacup. "The most eligible man in all of Kilnorn has effortlessly made you the target for the hatred and envy of every woman you know."

Chapter Three

Gryphon
- four years ago -

MY NOSE SCRUNCHES in distaste as ale, sweat, and roasted meat mingle together. The music is merry and the company joyous as bodies sweep across the room in a perfectly synchronized dance. It's uncharacteristically hot for a room of such a grand size but no one appears to mind.

The weight on my shoulder shifts, a grunt of consciousness making its way to my ears. My back straightens as I strain to hear more. Silence greets me. It won't be long, though. Perhaps another ten more minutes before he comes to. I must act swiftly if my plan is to go smoothly.

Time is of the essence.

My eyes quickly dart across the room. It doesn't take long before I find whom I look for. He's nearly impossible to miss with that atrocious crown atop his head.

I don't waste time.

The dancing bodies are little more than twigs in my way as I cross the room. Soft gasps and small screams of women unintentionally send their suitors after me on their behalf. A hand grips me roughly around the bicep before he yanks me.

"At minimum you owe Miss Rad—"

My eyes cut to him, a snarl pulling at my upper lip as an uncontrollable hatred seeps through my gaze. What a foolish man to so boldly grab hold of a beast.

The growl is low, rumbling through the inner workings of my chest and I fight off the urge to let it roar.

The man takes a step back, uncertainty washing over his face as his hand falls away from my arm. His eyes glance at the body thrown over my shoulder, his eyebrows furrowing as he takes a cautionary step backwards.

"I," he begins to say but I don't waste my time as I turn on my toes and walk away. He is nothing more than a fly, a nuisance in the greater scheme of things.

I continue on my way towards the king. There are two guards stationed within twenty feet of him and they easily catch sight of my determined approach. Without hesitation, they draw their swords and flank their king. The corner of my mouth quirks up. Two men against one beast? It's practically laughable.

"Halt!" one of the guards shouts.

That draws the king's attention. His hazy gaze and rosy cheeks tell me all I need to know. He may be too inebriated to understand my proposition but I cannot turn back now. I've already wasted a year and I am no closer to owning that town than I was the day I met *her*. I'll force the king to understand.

"I said halt," the guard repeats but my stride only quickens.

"Your Highness," my words are foreign on my lips, the disdain dripping off them like blood droplets from a still warm corpse. The king fails to hear any unkindness in my tone.

"I present to you my gift," I declare before tossing down the unconscious body.

"My God, is that…" the king trails off as he steps forward to get a better look.

My foot reaches out, shifting the head to the side so the king can see better.

"It *is*," the king practically hisses as his eyes snap up to mine. "Is he dead?"

"Not yet, Your Highness."

"Well, why the Hell not?"

"The request of my reward requires a… demonstration of sorts," I tell him. Then after a moment, I amend, "A private one."

The king arches up an eyebrow upon hearing that. I can see the disdain overtaking his drunken expression. Who am I to order him around? He is the king, the most powerful man in the entire country, yet here I am demanding a private audience with him. If it were not for the unconscious body at my feet, he'd order those swords be stabbed straight through my stomach. Thankfully, my mother taught me better. I'm no fool. I came prepared.

The king's finger taps along the side of his wine goblet as his lips purse to the side of his face.

"Your name."

It is not a question but a demand.

"Gryphon Pike."

His eyes narrow. "I've never heard your name. Who is your father?"

"Hawthorne Pike," I answer despite knowing he's never heard of the man.

We Pike men keep to ourselves, living on the outskirts of civilization. The beast within us holds no love for society. It was a miracle Father ever found a woman foolish enough to live her life with him. He could offer her nothing more than a wooden shack in the woods, but Mother loved him fiercely with all she had until the day he passed.

"Another man I know nothing about," the king grumbles to himself as his eyes narrow. "Yet you demand a private audience with your king? I ought to throw you in the dungeons—"

"A mistake if I ever heard one," I interrupt and his face flushes a deeper red. I continue speaking before he can order my head removed from my shoulders. "My services are best used within the wild, Your Highness. Not behind bars."

I tap my foot against the unconscious man, highlighting my talents. My words and my results give him pause. I'm sure there are many things he could use someone with my special talents for.

The man on the floor groans as he shifts, little wisps of consciousness finding their way back to him. My eyebrow arches as I stare down at the man before lifting my gaze to the king. *Well?* I ask him without words.

The king snaps his fingers before pointing down at the unconscious man. As if sharing one singular brain, the guards hoist the man up by his arms with little to no effort.

"Your demonstration," the king slurs as he makes his way towards the exit of the room.

Wordlessly, I follow after him, the two guards, and my prey. My footsteps are heavy as my heart races within my chest. Never in all my years have I willingly shown someone my gift, my curse. The unease winds down my spine, coilingly tightly around my stomach as bile races to the back of my throat.

The king may very well kill me for the truth I plan to show him. If that is the case, I'll have to kill him before he makes the command. That will be easy enough. It's the escaping that will be difficult. The guards will surely kill a wolf of my size, seeing it for the monster that I am. Even if they never find me the man, they will kill me the beast for fear of the damage I will cause. They may never understand what happened or how their king came to die by such a massive beast, but that will matter not. They'll exact their revenge on the wolf the moment the king dies. So yes. Escaping from here will prove quite difficult if it comes to that. I pray that it doesn't.

Trepidation fills my body as we silently walk down a hallway before entering a study. It's as grand and grotesque as one would expect of a king.

My jaw tightens as the door closes behind me. The guards discard the unconscious man on the floor and the king waves them off. A moment later, the guards exit the study. I didn't expect he'd truly allow himself to be alone. A fool for thinking himself invincible, but I will take it. The less people who know, the less people I will have to kill.

The guards exit the room just as the man gains consciousness. His hands instinctively go to his head and face. Grunts and groans tumble out of him as I assume he attempts to piece together the events.

Bleary eyes blink open, settling on the king as he stares viciously down at the man.

"Your Highness?"

The king offers a deeply pleased chuckle. "Yes."

"How... what am I... I do not understand," the man states and it is within this moment I realize the man does not know who he is.

A bastard son who holds too much power. The previous late king had many dalliances with the women of his court and King Byron has done his best to kill any offspring he learns of. It wasn't easy figuring out what would please a king who can buy whatever he desires but his father bestowed a gift upon me by being unable to keep his dick within his pants.

"Why am I here? Have I offended you in some way?" the man asks as he rubs his face.

"You? No," the king replies but he offers little else. A moment later his eyes snap to mine. "Well?"

I step towards the king, hesitation swarming within me but I force out the words. This is all for *her*. If it means exposing my secret to claim what is mine, then so be it.

"I offer my services to you for one full year," I state, eyes unwavering as I hold his drunken gaze. "In return, I desire the title Duke of Kilnorn."

"*Duke?*"

A moment later, the king's head falls back as he laughs so loudly that I wince. It's sharp and too grating for even a regular man. I should kill him if only to rid this world of such an atrocious sound.

"You? A nobody whose family name I've never heard?"

"My services are well worth more than the duke title," I state, red slowly bleeding into my vision.

I may be a beast but I am also a prideful man. I do not take kindly to being insulted. I may not be someone within his court, but I am certainly not *nobody*. He will soon come to understand that.

He openly scoffs. "I think not. No one of your stature has ever risen to dukedom in a single generation and I cannot fathom that ever occurring. I don't care what talents you have. You will *never* become a duke. Your son's son's son's *son* perhaps, but never you."

"I assure you, your position will change after you see what I can do," is all I say.

Bones crunch as my body shifts. Black fur scatters across my skin. I fall forward onto four paws as an elongated maw protrudes from my face. I despise shifting. The pain is almost never worth it, but for *her* I will do anything. *She* saw the man within the beast and offered a kindness I have never known. *She* is worth it all.

Growls and grunts echo off the walls as the transformation completes itself.

The king drops his wine goblet as terrified eyes stare down at me. I shake out of my torn clothes before settling my gaze on the man. His eyes are wide, his breathing clipped as he remains on the floor frozen in fear.

I look to the king, then back at the man before once more at the king. Realization dawns on the king's face and he offers me one curt, stiff nod. I act without hesitation.

I pounce.

Teeth sink into flesh as a gurgled, pain filled scream pierces the air. Copper blood coats my tongue as my teeth shred into the man's throat. He dies quickly, body going limp as warm blood pumps out of his exposed artery.

I drop him haphazardly to the ground, blood dripping out of my open mouth. I've never enjoyed the taste. A true oddity considering my background. Father loved it. So much so he craved Mother's flesh and blood. To the point where one day, he found himself with a bullet in his head, his love for her no longer more powerful than his desire to consume her.

I shift back, fur disappearing beneath pale skin as my paws shift to hands and feet. An ugly scar cuts across my left wrist. A painful yet beautiful reminder of *her*.

Sluggishly, I rise to my feet. Blood covers my chin, neck and chest, the taste lingering on my tongue as I spit out as much of it as I can.

"I offer you an untraceable killer for one full year," I tell him, not at all bothering to hide my immodesty. "In return, you give me Kilnorn."

The king is silent as he mulls over my proposition. "The Duke of Kilnorn?"

"Yes."

"Why?"

Why so small? I can practically hear him ask. Why not ask for a larger, grander life? I have a power none other possess. With it, I could own the country if I played my cards right. But that is not what I am after. I only desire to own *her*.

"I detest the grandiose nature of this culture," I tell him bluntly, not bothering to mince words. "Yet wealth and title are what I require for a luxurious life. Kilnorn is remote. The people are secluded and dreary. It is an uneventful town."

"Oddly perfect for what you desire," he says skeptically.

"Only a fool would come unprepared to speak with the king."

He clicks his tongue as his eyes shift down to the mangled corpse. "You can do this at will?"

"Yes."

"A wolf to deal with all my headaches," he muses to himself, hand coming to rub his chin. A thought occurs to him. I see it the moment it happens. A scowl grabs hold of his features and his eyes meet mine. "I am the king. It is my right to openly kill whomever I please. There is no one more powerful than me. What use do I have for hiding my intent?"

What he says doesn't surprise me. His father was brutal and as such, raised brutal children. So brutal they killed one another off until only Byron was left and when he grew impatient, he killed his father. But Byron has inherited many of the previous king's enemies and his own brutality has done nothing to thwart them. He'll need someone like me to if he wishes to keep his power.

"A murderous king collects many enemies," I reply and his face scrunches in thought.

He mulls over my statement, eyes settling back on the dead man. On his *half—brother*. He's been killing his siblings for too many years to count. Eventually it will catch up to him. Any one of those unnecessary deaths he's created could be the one to undo him.

"I suppose they do," he mumbles. "Very well. I will retain your services for a full year. In return, I will name you the Duke of Kilnorn. But hear me now, Gryphon Pike. If I so much as catch a scent of betrayal from you, your head will sit on a pike outside my gates.

"I plan to ride you hard and fast, dirty and raw. I will hear no words of complaint, no questions for a break. I will work you to the bone, so ask yourself, is Duke of Kilnorn worth the sacrifice?"

Pale blue eyes, a freckled face, and fiery orange hair flash through my mind. A face set in fierce determination to free a massive beast despite the danger it possessed to her being. Harsh, cruel words drowning in kindness. *I better not see you tomorrow... or I will finish the job.*

Is it worth it?

She is worth it.

"Yes, Your Highness. Duke of Kilnorn is worth it."

Chapter Four

Elvira
- present day -

FORKS CLINK AGAINST plates as the room practically suffocates in silence. Mother and Father refuse to look up from their food, a strange somberness overshadowing their features. Unease disrupts my stomach as I idly push my food around my plate.

Normally, Father would be telling us about his day, about how well the business is going or that we might brace ourselves for a difficult month. Yet he dares not open his mouth for anything other than food.

I swallow thickly as I glance between the two, my heartbeat picking up pace as I dare to interrupt the silence. Clumsily, I clear my throat.

"H—how did your day fare, Father?"

His entire body stiffens. My mother gazes briefly at him before bending her head downward to hide her expression. The hair along my arms and neck rise as my stomach clenches. I could never anticipate the words he's about to speak. They hit me like a ton of bricks.

"Four orders were cancelled today," he states, voice trembling as he attempts to keep his rage in check. "It would appear a witch has enchanted the new Duke of Kilnorn."

My stomach bottoms out as my heart all but stops. One simple word filled with such hatred and animosity. One simple word to turn my world upside down. One simple word to ruin the rest of our lives.

Witch.

Witch.

Witch.

My lips part but no words form. Four orders will affect the next two months, but the worst is yet to come. As word spreads like wildfire of my sinful deed, no new orders will be placed with Father. His business will dry up and we'll fail to make enough money to get us through the winter.

"Tell me, dear daughter," Father begins as he raises his angered, brown eyes to my pale blue ones. "Might you undo this enchantment?"

The shock of his words silence any reply I might have. My gaze cuts to Mother but she remains dutifully uninvolved. She refuses to raise her eyes from her plate, shoulders stiff as she pushes her food around rather than eating it.

My attention returns to Father, his eyes unforgiving and harsh. It is unclear to me if he believes I'm a witch, but his gaze speaks volumes. He believes me in enough power to dispel these ridiculous rumors. If only that were true.

"I—I cannot," I concede, a strange flush taking over my face at the admittance. "As soon as he entered the café he looked as though he was hunting someone and then his eyes found mine... It was discomforting. I don't know why he approached me. I've nothing to offer him. Not beauty nor charm nor talent. If I could undo it, I would, Father. Please believe me."

He huffs indignantly, fork and knife clattering against his plate as his hands raise to rub his forehead. My heart breaks. Defeat. Absolute defeat washes over him.

"Four orders," he mumbles. "Cancelled all because these miserable people believe a red headed woman *must* be a witch. We're not going to survive the winter."

That snaps Mother out of her solitude. Her hand immediately finds his forearm.

"We will," she assures him, but he refuses to look at her, his hands rubbing his forehead so roughly his skin turns red. "Just as we survived the ones that came before. We will survive this, Hunter."

"Eventually our luck will run out, Corvina," he replies, his arms thumping against the table as he glances at her. "Three mouths were difficult enough to feed when one of them was only a babe, but now..."

"Then cut my portions," I interject, fingers curling so tightly around my utensils they turn stark white. My heart beats as fast as a rabbit against my chest as I hold my father's striking eyes. "You shouldn't have to suffer my consequences."

Mother openly frowns while Father smiles sadly. It's as if they hold the same internal thought but it evokes a different emotion within them. I see it clear as day upon their faces and I suddenly feel so much like the child they see me as.

"Such a noble daughter," Father breathes out. "What a shame, then, that you were cursed with such appearances."

Words so harsh and kind, filled with such abundant love yet devastating loss. My heart lurches within my chest and it pains me as I swallow around the lump in my throat. How cruel this world can be. Through no fault of my own I bear the marks of a witch, though in my many years, I've come to understand a witch can look like any woman so long as enough people dislike her.

No matter how hard I try, no matter the shapes I try to bend myself into, the people of Kilnorn will always hate me. *Red headed witch* has cursed me my entire life. It has cast me out, shunned me, and banned me from even the simplest life. Yet they believe me capable enough, powerful enough to enchant the duke? When I cannot even save my family from destitution?

Father inhales deeply, steeling himself as he looks to me, then Mother. "We must brace ourselves for a difficult winter. If this is the one to claim us, it won't be without a fight."

Mother and I remain silent, but we offer him firm, determined nods of agreement. If we are to go down, we will go down fighting.

"I WORRY FOR LYDIA, planning that ball all by herself," Annalise declares as we take a stroll through Main Street. "News of the duke's temperament does not paint him as a kindly man."

Cold, crisp air cuts through the street, a heavy dampness swirling within. Mud lines the streets, trapping carriages within the side alleys off the main road. Kilnorn has been far too poor and out of the king's good graces to have each road cobbled. But not the main road. It has always been pristinely maintained, the pride and joy of the dreary and drab Kilnorn.

Today is no different with potted plants and flowers bursting with life and color despite the gray, cloudy sky.

The cobblestone road has been swept and brushed of debris and mud from yesterday's storm. Any storefronts that required a touch up received it in the early hours of the morning. All in all, Main Street is the exact opposite of what Kilnorn is truly like. Colorful and bursting with life.

"How is the duke's temperament?" I ask as I do my best to avoid the glares being thrown my way.

Stares of sympathy and pity reach Annalise while vitriol and disdain are reserved decidedly for me. With her appealing features and demure character, the people of Kilnorn see her friendship with the witch as one full of pious ignorance of a young woman. Some days, I can't help but agree.

"It's wicked," Annalise answers in a hushed whisper. "Surely she cannot be safe within his presence. Not someone of her... pedigree."

"And what of her pedigree?" I ask, unsure if she means what I believe she does.

Lydia and her family are far more educated than the most educated people within Kilnorn. They exude class, etiquette, and a kindness unknown to Kilnorn. Yet the shortsightedness of Kilnorn's people and its distance from the capital city has delayed our town's progressiveness.

The late King Byron, for all his faults, had done one good deed decades before his untimely death and that was allowing *all* peoples of his kingdom the access to wealth, nobility, and status regardless of the color of the skin, the shape of their eyes, or uncommon features such as a missing limb from birth.

Yet Kilnorn, who believes a red headed woman *must* be a witch, cannot share in the king's or capital's acceptance. If Lydia and her family were not as well educated as they were, if they had not obtained such wealth before it was unfortunately lost when their business took a hit, if they lacked the proper etiquette in any degree, Kilnorn would have either chased them from the city or made it impossible for them to ever show their faces.

"All I meant is that the duke will be far less likely to accept her the way you and I have. Not with that temper of his."

"As he hails from Edlercross, I suspect he may be far more accepting of her than anyone in Kilnorn," I counter, voice curt and brusque. With a sentence like that, she knows full well of what she says. How could she speak so cruelly about someone she calls her friend?

I know they are not close friends, but I always thought they were friends enough. If they truly hated one another, how could they spend so much time in each other's presence? But now my naivety is being plucked from me. If Annalise truly thought Lydia a friend, she would never speak so crudely about something Lydia has no control over.

I don't mince words as I continue to speak. "I feel that I should remind you, Annalise, people of her *pedigree* are within the king's court and ruling class. There is also the matter that the duke did not hesitate to hire her. He appeared rather unaware and unbothered by her *pedigree*. Unlike you."

Annalise's face flushes as she sputters her response. "*I* have no qualms with her pedigree. Lydia is a fine lady. His Grace is lucky to have her help in planning this ball. All I'm saying is I worry for her when he is such a brutish man."

I come to an abrupt stop, my conflicted feelings swirling within. Annalise has been my friend for as long as I can remember. The *only* friend I had until Lydia and her family moved to Kilnorn when I was at the ripe age of fifteen. Annalise stayed by my side despite the cruel treatment I received, despite her parents forbidding her from being my friend, despite her reputation being on the line. She remained loyal and faithful.

Yet it is difficult for me to turn a blind eye of her opinion and treatment towards Lydia. Lydia, who may have harsh words but only ever cares about my best interest. Lydia, who may have lost a life of luxury but always shares what little wealth she can spare with my family. Lydia, who cannot control the color of her skin or the treatment she receives but will always treat everyone like an equal until proven otherwise.

Two friends who have been a lifeline for me yet one of them painfully cannot see past her own ignorance and hatred.

"Elvira?"

My eyes snap to Annalise's questioning gaze and my stomach clenches. She has been a good friend to me for so many years. Has been a light within the darkness, but now *she* has become that same darkness for my dear friend Lydia.

"Annalise, I cannot..." my words trail off as I desperately search for how to say it. "Lydia is my *friend*. A dear one at that. I have been far too compliant in your treatment towards her despite knowing exactly how that feels. The people of Kilnorn cannot look past the color of my hair and you... you cannot look past the color of Lydia's skin. She is far more educated, far more talented, far more kind than either of us will ever be and yet you speak of her as though she deserves no consideration at all. I cannot... I *will not* stand by that any longer."

"Elvira," Annalise gasps, mouth falling open as shock grabs hold of her features. And then the anger bleeds out as her eyes narrow. I take a step back, so unused to seeing such a foul expression upon her face. It is anger, betrayal, and poison. She holds nothing back.

"I have stayed by your side, *loyally*, when all others had banished you. I was your *only* friend. I did not have to be. No one would have blamed me if I stopped being your friend, but I remained. I offered you my kindness and my friendship and this is how I am rewarded for remaining so foolishly loyal?"

"There are no rewards for friendship, Annalise," I reply, my heart a thundering mess as my fingers curl into my palms. Tears burn my eyes as a reality I never considered is shoved down my throat. I choke on it, on the words as I force them out. "The friendship itself *is* the reward. Heaven above, Annalise, have you ever *liked* me or have you always been chasing some sort of praise from the people of Kilnorn for your abundant kindness?"

I cannot believe the words of my insecurity have finally left my mouth. Neither can Annalise as she takes a small step back from me, shock written all over her demeanor. Her hand covers her mouth, her eyes wide as she shields her body from me by angling it away.

"I will not justify that with a response," she breathes out as her hand falls away from her mouth. "I will do you the courtesy of pretending I never even heard it."

A stab of pang hits my heart at the unshed tears within her eyes. Have I spoken too rashly? Perhaps Annalise truly is concerned for Lydia's wellbeing. Perhaps she worries he might prey upon her in some sick, twisted way he would not prey upon women such as us. Perhaps my desire to pretend there is nothing different between Lydia and I has shrouded me in blindness.

"Annalise—"

She shakes her head, taking another step from me. "I have other errands to attend to. Have a good day."

She spins abruptly before hastily walking away. A cold wind blows through the street, running a chill down my spine as I watch my friend create a distance between us that is far more than physical.

"Should I be concerned by that parting?" Lydia's smooth voice interrupts my thoughts.

Whirling around surprised, I find her a few short steps from me. Her head is held high, her shoulders pulled taut in perfect posture. Dark brown eyes study me intently, lips pursing slightly. Her hands rest gently in front of her waist, delicate and refined. She exudes elegance and class that is so foreign to Kilnorn. She was *born* for Edlercross. Kilnorn is merely a momentary stop for her before she returns to her rightful place.

"No," I answer her after several moments. "A minor spat, I assure you."

"There was nothing minor about that, Elvira," Lydia states knowingly as if she heard the words ripped from my mouth.

My brain stalls, unsure of how to respond to her cutting words. Instead, I simply change the topic.

"How is the ball coming along?"

Her eyebrow quirks momentarily, giving away some inner thought she surely wished remained hidden, but she plays along well enough. Allows me the change of topic

"His Grace has given me free reign," she answers simply. "Without any interjections, the ball is coming along nicely. You better brush up on your planning, Elvira, if you wish not to drown."

My eyebrows furrow together. "Why would I—"

"Honestly, Elvira, have you no desire to obtain his hand?" Lydia snaps, frustration slicing across her face. "He *fancies* you. Use that. Earn his deeper affections. Think of what that'll mean for you, for your family."

"He fancies me because he does not know me or my reputation as a witch. Soon enough, his interest will be as if it were never there to begin with."

"That is not true. His Grace fancies you because you are beautiful but this wretched town will have you believe otherwise. He is not daft like the people of Kilnorn. He is enraptured by what he sees. You must seize this opportunity before the vultures descend upon him and take his attention away."

"They'll descend anyway," I argue weakly, not believing the words she speaks. I know she believes them but that doesn't make them true. "He'll find a more suitable lady deserving of his title. Someone like you, Lydia. Marry him and take him back to Edlercross."

"I have no interest in him," she replies curtly.

"No, but you certainly have interest in his ten thousand rysar and no one is more deserving of his money than you."

She smiles, not vindictive or coy, but affectionately as if she's letting me in on a sacred secret. Her hand reaches out, gently grabbing hold of mine as her soft fingers give my hand a light squeeze. When she speaks, her words are firm while her eyes shine. She parts a wisdom I do not fully understand.

"If I teach you one thing before I leave this dreadful place, it is this. *Never* settle, Elvira. Not when you can have the world."

Chapter Five

Gryphon

- one year ago -

RAGE BURNS THROUGH me hot as embers as my boots echo through the corridor. Candle lit flames dimly light the hallway I've become *too* familiar with. Guards are stationed evenly apart, unconcerned by my presence as I storm the halls. They all know my face by now and have deemed me an unworthy threat.

King Byron's orders echo within my head. *You are to kill Earl Lucius within the week. Only then will you have earned your dukedom.* The bastard has been withholding my title for far too long. No more. No more will I postpone owning Kilnorn, owning *her*. The King should never have toyed with the beast. Now, he will reap what he sows.

I turn down the hall, my steps sure. There are no rooms within the castle that I am unfamiliar with. No secret halls or servant entrances I am unaccustomed with. I know them all. Intimately. For this *exact* purpose.

Eagerly, I slip behind velvet curtains, my hand pressing into the sigil that unlocks the painting. It creaks against its hinges but I do not care about the noise. Swiftness is prized over stealth in a place as grand and large as the castle. Noises ghost down these hallways more times than I care to count. What is one more of creaky hinges among many?

The hallway is dark and damp. It takes a moment for my eyes to adjust to the darkness, but I'm soon stalking the narrow hall with renewed vigor. Spider webs and dust tickle my senses as I cut through the inner workings of the castle. I turn left, then right. Up a questionable ladder. It threatens to break beneath my weight but I am disappearing down the hall before it has the chance.

Finally, I reach the door. It pops open and I slip out into the darkened room. A figure rests within the large bed, his breaths calm and even. Asleep. I do not hesitate. My legs carry me quickly across the room. My hand grabs him roughly by the shoulder and I give him a shake.

He shouts as he flails around in the bed. I can see the moment his mouth begins to form the word *guards* but he's silenced quickly by my hand. He fights me, fingers curling around my wrist as he attempts to yank me off him. It's no use. A man is too weak for the beast that I am.

"Stop fighting and I will release you," I growl low and quiet.

He stills instantly, recognition befalling his features as he nods his head once. When he doesn't move for a few more seconds, I remove my hands from him. He sits up quickly, throwing the blankets off him as he walks across the room towards the candles, *not* the exit, and lights a few.

"To what do I owe this pleasure?" he asks, voice groggy from sleep but not any less sharp.

He turns, leveling me with dark green eyes as his chestnut hair falls in his face. He's uncharacteristically fit for someone of his stature. Unlike his family who indulges themselves in the gluttony of their wealth, he's more reserved. He lacks the rounded belly of his father, the lethargic nature of his older brother, the addiction of his mother. His mind remains far too sharp and aware but that is precisely why I've sought him out and no one else.

"You know of my deal with your father," I state.

It's not a question. I know he knows. I don't know *how* he knows but I no longer care. He knows what I can do and that is great use for me now.

"I might," he answers with an air of reserve, like he doesn't want to give away all his secrets and leverage.

A smart man. I was right to come to him.

"I am extending that deal to you instead," I say.

His eyebrows shoot up towards his hairline, the flame of the candle flickering against his face. Intrigue dances within his eyes.

"How, exactly, does that work?"

"I remove the obstacles within your way," I answer him bluntly. There's no point in mincing words. "When it is done, I leave with the title Duke of Kilnorn."

"Not quite," he states as he sits down in a chair.

He's too elegant in his movements, too refined. Like every move is filled with too much purpose. I suppose that happens to a person when too many eyes are constantly watching and waiting for your failure.

My teeth clench tightly at his opposition.

"Then what do you propose?" I grind out.

"You remove the obstacles in my way. You are free to live in Kilnorn as the duke *but* I shall keep you on retainer whenever the need arises. Indefinitely."

A mind too sharp and aware, indeed. It's a shame, really, that he was second born and not first. His brother resembles their father too much. They believe they're invincible, that no one would dare to conspire against them all because of the title they own and the crown they wear atop their heads.

Foolish, idiotic people. That is precisely why this plan shall work. The king would never dream I'd move against him. He'd believe his sons would but not his mindless beast.

"I agree to your conditions," I answer swiftly. His terms are far more agreeable than what I've been subjected to. I may not desire to be on retainer till the day I die, but I *must* have Kilnorn. I can wait no longer. "But if you threaten the life I lead in Kilnorn—"

"I wouldn't dream of it Mr. Pike," he laughs out in a low chuckle. "I'm fully aware that the beast, if provoked, will bite the hand that feeds it. Kilnorn is yours as soon as the crown is mine."

I don't doubt his words. Perhaps I should, considering how his father has betrayed me, but he's too smart. He will honor our deal. He will do his best to keep me happy as that's in his best interest. After all, he knows that a happy beast is a loyal beast.

"When would you like me to do it?"

"I require time," he confesses as he crosses one leg over the other, his eyes going distant as he thinks of the upcoming coup. "There are a lot of moving pieces I must put into place. I will let you know when you are free to move."

"Understood," I say as I start to head towards the private entrance to his room.

"Mr. Pike," he calls to me and I turn to face him. "Have patience. It will be months before I am ready. You will have to remain his dog a little longer, I'm afraid."

A snarl rips apart my mouth as my eyes narrow at him. "If you drag this out too long, I will turn my sights on you, Silas."

He smiles wide and deep, far too amused for a man —a *prince*— who's just had his life threatened.

"Oh, I don't doubt it," he hums, not showing an ounce of fear despite the beast standing before him. "Give me a year. I'll be ready within the year."

"Understood," I gruffly reply.

"I look forward to our lasting relationship, Mr. Pike," he calls to me as I disappear into the hidden hallways. "Great things are about to come."

- *one month ago* -

THE AIR IS HEAVY as I maneuver the thick brush of the woods. Gray clouds cover the sky, shielding the sun fully from view. Rain threatens to unleash its rage but luck remains on our side. Rain would cut their hunting trip short. We cannot have that. Not when all the pieces have finally aligned perfectly in place.

In one afternoon, I will finally have all that I have desired.

Kilnorn.

Dukedom.

Her.

The blood within my veins buzzes in delight. Soon it will all be mine.

Horses neigh in the distance, alerting me of their presence. I crouch lower into the brush, hiding my black fur and large body as best I can. King Byron has no idea what lurks ahead. Years of his torture are finally going to be repaid. My lips peel back in a smile as I wait for them to get closer.

"Pull the dogs back," Silas's voice carries through the forest. "They'll scare the prey."

"What prey?" his older brother asks, all the haughtiness he possesses dripping in those two words.

"I saw a pheasant lurking this way," Silas answers without missing a beat.

My heart pounds within my chest, the excitement vibrating within every bone I possess. A distant thud echoes off the ground, followed shortly by a second. Good. They've dismounted their horses.

"Father, will you not be joining us?" Silas asks.

"Pheasants are a waste of time," King Byron replies, his words slurring together.

A low growl emits from my chest against my wishes and birds scatter towards the sky. The hunting party goes silent for a few moments, their movements stilled as they attempt to hear more of the beast that lurks within the forest beside them. I shift lower into the brush.

"And what of a wolf?" Silas asks and I can practically hear him smiling.

"You don't have one in your study yet," his brother states, unknowingly encouraging his father towards his death. "It would look good mounted on the wall, wouldn't you agree?"

"Yes. It would."

A moment later, another thud hits the earth. How fitting. He hunts the wolf that hunts him. Let us see who wins today.

They stalk the forest, their feet as quiet as they can carry them against dead leaves and brush. I slink forward only far enough to catch sight of them. The king haphazardly carries his weapon as he sways on his feet.

His eldest son looks around the forest with wide and wild eyes. And Silas trails too far behind them, weapon carefully held within his hands as he searches for me. Does he fear I might turn on him after killing his father and brother? A smart man to be so cautious but it's unnecessary. I cannot gain my status as Duke of Kilnorn without royalty. He is safe.

For now.

I offer another low growl to keep their interest. The brother jumps, hands tightening around his weapon as he holds it too close to his chest. The king brightens, a little yip falling out of his mouth.

"This way, this way," King Byron urges them, heading loosely towards me.

I edge away from the king, wanting to attack from behind. His steps fumble in his drunken state. Expertly, I circle around him. As I do, my eyes catch sight of Silas, of his watchful dark green gaze as he stops walking altogether. He looks every bit like the king his father should have been. Poised. Regal. *Dangerous*.

Silas Ambrose the Third is not one I can so easily betray.

He takes a few steps back, his brother and father utterly unaware of what hunts them. I nearly laugh at their stupidity. Their own hubris has led to their downfall. I'd pity them if I didn't hate them so much. They've made my life a living Hell these past few years. The king did so in an attempt to remind me of who truly holds the power and his eldest son... he did it because he's too stupid to realize power doesn't come from a title. The world will not mourn their egos nor their deaths. And I will finally have the freedom I've been promised.

I attack without hesitation.

My teeth sink into the supple flesh between King Byron's shoulder and neck. Blood pools within my mouth, warm and thick in iron. A scream full of pain and agony bursts out of him. He falls to his knees the moment I release him.

Barely a moment later, my attention turns towards his eldest son. He shouts, raising the weapon towards me, but before he is able to fire one off, my jaw clamps down around his throat. My teeth sink into him as easily as a hot knife against smooth butter.

The tension of his skin pops and blood gushes out of him. His strangled gargles fill the forest. He's dead a few moments later.

Scuffled feet against dried leaves draw my attention. King Byron aims his weapon at me, rage filling his gaze as he recognizes the unnatural size of me.

I yank his son forward, his body taking the brunt of the weapon as the king shoots. The king wastes no time as he readies to shoot again but it's useless when I leap on him, my teeth tearing into him overzealously. *You should never have withheld what belongs to me.* His skin shreds easily but I don't let up. Not until his body is a mangled mess, nearly unidentifiable.

Footsteps snap me out of my rage and I see Silas walking towards me. His eyes are guarded but his steps are sure. He stops a foot from me, head barely bowed due to my massive height. Wordlessly, he offers me his arm. My head tilts sideways as I stare at him.

"I cannot start my reign with uncertainty," he states. "Do not harm me but leave your mark."

A rough nod of my head is all he receives before I lunge at him. He flops, hard, against the unforgiving ground as my teeth raze his clothes. I maul him as gently as I can. He is little more than a ragdoll in my strong jaws. It would be too easy to end his life. He recognizes that fact, fear shining within those guarded green eyes, but he does not recoil. He allows me to toss him around, my bite rough yet gentle.

After several prolonged moments, I release him, stepping back and offering him space. He lays there for a few short seconds before rising up. His clothes are destroyed, a few pink and red marks along his skin but no blood. He's clearly been attacked but blessed by the gods. Unlike his father and brother.

My bones crunch and snap as I shift forms. Blood coats my mouth, chin, and chest as I rise up onto my bare feet. Silas studies me, studies the transition the way a scientist would. No disgust or fear within his gaze. Only morbid curiosity.

"It is done," I state, my voice hoarse as I stand before him naked and bare. "Kilnorn is mine."

"Yes it is," he answers without hesitation. "In one month."

My eyes flash wild as I take a threatening step towards him. He raises a hand, feet firmly planted on the ground, never once shying away from my approach. A brave man. A stupid man.

"I have two members of the royal family to bury and a coronation to plan. I cannot anoint you as a duke until the coronation is complete. Then you will have your city... and whoever resides there that you so desire."

My blood turns to ice as a growl, low and threatening, ripples through me. Too smart and aware, indeed. King Byron bought my lie the moment I supplied it, never questioning such a simple answer. Silas is not his father. He might already know exactly who I am after and if he doesn't, he surely intends to find out.

"If you interfere with what is mine—"

"Relax, Gryphon Pike. I benefit from your services too much to jeopardize them so recklessly like that but hear this loud and clear. I will use this person against you if you so much as attempt to move against me. I am not stupid nor foolish like my father. I will know if you make moves and you'll know when I make mine because it will be too late for you. We have a fortuitous relationship. Let us not sully it."

"You have my word so long as I have yours."

A smile spreads across his lips. His hand rests atop his heart as he holds my gaze boldly without fear and without the invincibility King Byron held on to too tightly.

He is the king his father should have been.

"And you have my word so long as I have yours, Gryphon Pike."

Silence drapes around us as the first droplets of rain hit us. We hold each other's gazes quietly until the rain is a downpour. Finally, I relent. I offer him a bow.

"Congratulations on your ascension, King Silas."

He chuckles as I begin my transformation back into the beast. His eyes dance with fervor and excitement. King had been too far removed from him due to his birthright, yet now with the death of his father and brother, it is his. He's nothing more than a boy finally receiving the toy he's always wanted.

"And to you, Duke of Kilnorn," he hums. "A wolf in sheep's clothing will do us both good."

I will never be able to truly pass as one of his noblemen and Silas understands that all too well. My nature is too brusque, too wild, too unforgiving. Yet I know that is not what he speaks of. A literal wolf among humans. Indeed, he will benefit from it greatly.

And so long as he maintains his word, so will I.

Chapter Six

Elvira
- present day -

THE TOWN IS STRANGLED in excitement as the ball quickly approaches yet I cannot find it within me to care. Three more orders have been cancelled and no new ones have been placed. Father's business is decimated. He's been forced to close up shop or else look like a fool. The ball is the least of my concerns but it's impossible to ignore.

It lurks behind every corner, every whisper, every laughter. The people of Kilnorn haven't had a celebration like this in years. The previous duke held no great pleasure in hosting balls for the townsfolk. He rather enjoyed watching us suffer in our misery while he sat in his estate hoarding his wealth. Certainly no one can blame us for the excitement we bear towards the ball.

No one, no matter how young or old, would dare miss the event. No one except for my family. Not even taking into consideration our lack of finances, no one *wants* us there. Especially not me, the wicked witch come to tempt the Duke of Kilnorn from all the other deserving young, fertile women. I'd been so foolish to hastily agree to His Grace's proposition. Now, I fear I'll make him look a fool by not attending his event.

"Elvira," Father's voice cuts across the living space as he stands near the door. "Are you expecting any suitors?"

My head snaps over towards him, eyes wide as I stand up from the worn couch.

"None at all," I answer him quickly but my feet remain frozen where I stand.

Mother, however, is as light as a sparrow, darting across the space in record time so that she can saddle up beside Father. He leans out of her way, allowing her entry into his small space as they gawk outside the window from behind a torn curtain.

"Maybe he's lost," Mother muses as her hands rest along Father's back and arm.

"He seems rather sure in his steps," Father hums in response. "Not many homes out this way."

"That is precisely why his steps are sure," Mother argues. "With so few homes nearby, he must be in need of our hospitality. Quickly, Elvira, tidy up the place as best you can. He looks wealthy."

That snaps me out of my stupor and I hurriedly do as she ordered. Our home may not be grandiose enough for the wealthy, but we can keep it to a certain standard easily enough.

"Do you think he might be from the neighboring town?" I inquire as I shove linen underneath a bedframe.

"It's hard to say," Father murmurs. "He doesn't look like any of the men I know from Kilnorn."

"Nor any that I know," Mother states. "Quickly, quickly. He's approaching the door."

The three of us jump into action, our feet scuffling against the dirty, wooden floor. Father stands dutifully at the front door, eagerly waiting for the knock while Mother stands a few feet from him and me a few feet from her.

The excitement is practically tangible. We never receive guests. Not even Lydia's family, though they've attempted a few times. We would never insult them by inviting them to our abysmal abode.

Firm boots thud against our stoop before three strong raps shake the door against its frame. Father jolts, sending a gasp out of my and Mother's mouth. He shoots us a look, equal parts amusement and apprehension, before his hand clamps around the doorknob and he pulls it open.

"Yes, how might I help you?" Father asks in his business voice.

A smile touches my lips. It's been some time since I've had the pleasure of hearing him speak that way. I try to stay away from his place of business lest I remind people too often he is the father of a witch.

"Is this the Noire residence?" a gruff cadence penetrates the room and my back goes rigid.

I cannot see him from the way Father has positioned the door but I can never forget the brusqueness of his voice nor the abrupt way he speaks. His Grace Gryphon Pike stands on my stoop.

"Yes it is," Father answers. "How might I help you?"

"Your daughter. Elvira Noire. I wish to call upon her."

Shock ripples through my father's body, his fingers turning white as he grips the door.

"Your Grace?" he ventures to ask. Father has yet to see the new duke, but with the rumors swirling around, it's easy to surmise whom might be inclined to call upon me.

"Yes."

Father's eyes cut towards me for the briefest of moments and then all too suddenly, he falls into the role of father and not businessman. A peculiar look overcomes his features, one mixed between respect and protectiveness.

"You wish to call upon her *now?*"

"Yes."

"And what of a chaperone?"

Silence greets us and then, "A chaperon is needed?"

"*Yes,* Your Grace! I cannot have my daughter sullying her reputation by prancing around unattended in the presence of a male that is not her family. Surely you are aware of what that would mean for her."

More silence.

"We are in the woods," His Grace pointedly states, his patience wearing thing. "Who would see us so far from town?"

"That is not the point, Your Grace," Father replies exasperatedly and I cannot help the small giggle that bubbles out of my chest. "A chaperone is required for any unwed woman in the presence of a man—"

"Then *you* chaperone," His Grace cuts him off and my father actually sputters, his face turning red in indignation.

"I cannot! That is not for a man to do!"

"Oh, for fuck's sake," His Grace growls, the annoyance now flirting dangerously towards anger as he pushes his way into the house.

His hand is large upon the door, dwarfing my father's, as he shoves past Father. Greedy, wild amber eyes find me immediately and the tension that is coiled within his shoulders loosen.

His curly black hair falls into his eyes, pronouncing his crooked nose even more. The scar on the right side of his face seems softer today and I realize it is because he hasn't trimmed his ever growing facial hair.

The clothes upon his back are well tailored, high end cloth yet they look strange on his figure. Like he is merely playing the part of duke instead of embodying it. He's far too tall to be considered common, a fact I hadn't noticed back in the café. All the prying eyes had been a distraction, but now within the privacy of my own home, his towering, bulky frame is rather intimidating.

His eyes cut to Father, then Mother, before stating firmly, "You will chaperone us here."

"Of course," Mother replies before Father can rebuke. "Please sit, Your Grace. Elvira."

She nods her head towards the table, a stern expression on her face. The abrupt turn of events has my heart lodged firmly within my throat. We are hosting the Duke of Kilnorn within our pitiful home. What is it about this man that is so determined to make my acquaintance? Surely he's heard the rumors by now. Why would he associate himself with someone so publicly scorned? The townsfolk believe me a witch. Doesn't he care about that?

The sudden loudness of a chair scraping against the wooden floor snaps me to attention. His Grace stands behind the chair, eyes glued to me as he holds it out for me to sit in. He does not smile or greet me warmly. He's rather cold and distant. Not a single friendly ounce within him. The same as the other day within the café.

That strange nagging feeling of danger lurking beneath the surface prods at me but I shake it away. I cannot reject his offer, especially when we are within the confines of my home. There's nowhere for me to escape to.

Shyly, I sit in the chair he's offered me. He pushes me in, the action rough and unpracticed. As he pulls away, I catch sight of the state of his hands. Scarred and worn. He sits down rather ungracefully in the chair across from me. The chair is dwarfed by his massive size. His hands splay across the worn wooden table, his eyes searing into me as if he can see straight down to my soul.

My teeth snag on my lower lip as my gaze concentrates on the intricate grains of the table. His brusque nature and physical features remind me of what I already deduced a few days ago. He most certainly was never meant to be a duke. His hands are too calloused, his manners too rusty, and his conversation too abrupt.

If he were not meant to become a duke, how did he acquire such a title and wealth?

"Tea, Your Grace?" Mother asks as she places the kettle on the fire.

"It matters not," he states and my eyebrows pinch towards the center of my face. It's quite rude to reject hospitality. He catches the look before I can smother it away and clears his throat loudly. "Unless you have some to spare."

"Of course, Your Grace," Mother replies warmly as she retrieves two mugs.

"How are you finding Kilnorn, Your Grace?" Father asks as he sits down adjacent to us.

His Grace visibly bristles as he cuts a quick glare at Father before settling his gaze back on me.

"Does the question interest you?" he pointedly asks me.

After all, he came all this way specifically to see me. My father flushes another shade of red at His Grace's rudeness, but he has the good sense to remain quiet. I nod my head politely as I answer.

"It does, Your Grace."

"Gryphon," he exhales, mouth tight as his fingers curl towards the palm of his hand. "For all that is holy and good, I beg you do *not* call me Your Grace."

"That is a bit unusual, Your Grace," I state, discomfort shifting through me.

Most nobles refuse to shed their titles even when speaking to their families. His Grace and I have barely been acquainted. For him to request I refer to him by his given name... not even his *surname* but the one his parents bestowed upon him is too much.

His jaw clenches, eyes narrowing. "I do not wish to hear such a useless title from your lips. My name is what I desire to hear. It was good enough for my mother, it is good enough for you."

"*Useless* title?" I ask aghast.

How can he say such a thing while sitting in our squalor? The title duke would change our lives forever. We would never be left with starving bellies and shivering bodies. People would not scorn us so openly within the streets. The color of my hair would no longer matter. We would have wealth, status, and power over this town.

"Yes. Useless," he replies. "I'm still a dog attached to the king's leash, am I not? Aren't all the nobles within his kingdom? There's little freedom to boast about when I am at his every beck and call."

I've never heard a man talk so brazenly about the royal family before. Besides, I thought King Silas and His Grace were rather friendly with one another. Or so the rumors say.

"I'd rather a leash around my neck so long as the bed is warm and the bowl full," I state and his eyes flash.

"Careful what you say, Miss Noire. There are things much worse than the life you lead here."

"Then why did you accept the title Duke of Kilnorn? If you despise it so, I see no reason for why you would take it on."

His lips peel back, a strange satisfactory smirk upon his mouth as he stares at me with eyes reminiscent of a large beast I'd stumbled upon five years ago. It startles me so much I nearly jolt within my seat. The wolf had been eerily similar of man and now, this man before me, is eerily similar to the wolf.

"I accepted it," he states calmly yet each word drips with saccharine poison, "for you, little rabbit."

"But you've only just met me," I argue, my heart a thundering mess within my chest as my hair rises along my skin.

Father feels it too, the danger swimming beneath the surface. His back has gone stiff straight while he can't tear his eyes away from the duke. His hand curls atop his knee and I know he's wishing his weapon was within his hand.

The image of the wolf flashes through my mind again and for a moment, I swear the beast and the man are one and the same.

"You showed me a kindness that has been seared into my essence," he confesses as he leans back into his chair, a strange comfortableness seeping into his bones. "I doubt you remember. It was many years ago. It matters not."

He waves his hand dismissively, as if swatting away this shared memory we supposedly have. I cannot recall a time ever seeing His Grace prior to our meeting at the café. Could he have confused me with someone else? *Unlikely.* Not many people have hair like mine. Not a single person in Kilnorn besides myself has red hair. It came from my great, great grandfather on my mother's side. No one thought him a witch, though.

Unease drips down my spine as the silence drags on. His jaw tightens, eyes darting down my frame then back to my eyes. He leans forward over the table, his presence overwhelmingly large and suffocating as his dark amber eyes drink me in.

"You have inflicted upon me an illness I cannot cure without you," he states in that low, gruff voice, a hidden anger lacing every word.

"What if I do not desire to cure you?" I whisper, fear tightening its hold around my throat as my eyes cannot tear away from his.

His lips pull back, a snarl mixing in with his smile. "When you can have all that you desire, you dare shun it?"

"I've heard rumors of your temper—"

"Not for you, never for you," he quickly interrupts me, my words barely having left my mouth.

"Your Grace," Father begins cautiously, swallowing thickly as his eyes dart to mine, then Mother's before back to the duke. "Are you... concerned my daughter may have cast a spell on you?"

The duke's face morphs into deep confusion. The lines etched onto his face speak of hardship and pain as he gazes at my father with narrowed, questioning eyes.

"Witches lord no power over me," he states so casually my heart falters. He doesn't even realize the kindness he's spoken to me. "It is God I curse."

That small piece of information shocks me. Not many, especially someone within the king's circle, would so boldly and openly shun God.

"You're not a pious man, Your Grace?" I ask before I can think it through.

He barks out a rough laugh, the sound sharp yet deep. His amber eyes twinkle in delight as his index finger taps against the table. He stares at me, the edges of his lips quirking upwards.

"God wants no love of mine, Miss Noire," he answers before adding, "It's Gryphon to you."

"I could not—"

"You must," he interjects. "I insist."

"As my daughter stated previously, it's a bit of an unusual request. You've only just met—"

"It is our third meeting," he says. "I have earned it, have I not?"

"Well, I..." my father trails off, unsure how to respond to such oddity.

"As I do not recall our first meeting, it can only be counted as our second," I state curtly. If he hears how nervous my voice sounds, he does not mock me for it.

He arches up an eyebrow, a slow smile peeling back his lips. "Then I wholly expect to hear my name upon your lips at our third meeting, Miss Noire."

The sultriness of his voice has blood rushing to my cheeks and ears. I cannot stop myself from imagining what it might be like to kiss his mouth; to *feel* him the way his voice sounds and the way his eyes look as he gazes at me.

Instantly, my eyes cast away as a strange heat floods my stomach. My hands curl towards my palms as I pray God forgives me for such untoward thoughts.

"I do not make such promises, Your Grace," I reply, unable to meet his gaze.

He chuckles, low and deep, as he sits back in his chair. "No. You do not. Very well."

His eyes turn about the room, studying the faces of my parents, before he rises to his feet. Large, calloused hands tug the hem of finery. The thread strains against the largeness of His Grace's frame. He seems so out of place yet perfectly within place. A strange combination of a man. One seemingly used to such squalor with calloused hands and a rough appearance, yet the golden ring upon his pinky finger speaks of wealth and comfort. A strange, peculiar man and I cannot deny the intrigue he's sparked.

Golden eyes meet mine and the corner of his mouth curls up once more. "I will call upon you again, Miss Noire. I have no intentions of letting you slip away."

My manners escape me, my mouth hanging wide open as if to catch flies. My ears flare as a heat scorches my cheeks down to my bosom. The hair along the back of my neck rises as the meaning of his words sink in. No kind words of marriage, no proposals of courtship, no gentle admiration. He means to own me, to lock me up as his mistress, his wife, or his whore. Whichever one suits him best.

No other words are spoken as he offers Father a brief nod of his head, a curt, stiff half bow to Mother, and an unruly smile to me before he's out the door. Father is instantly at the door the moment His Grace has left. He barricades it with a chair, eyes wide, face a little pale, as he turns his attention to me.

"He is no man of God, Elvira," Father says, voice trembling as he braces the door.

"He is a *duke*," Mother reminds us, her hands clutched to her bosom as she stands halfway between Father and me. "We cannot refuse him."

"Then we move," Father states.

"With what money?" she asks him.

He curses because Mother is right. We have no means of leaving Kilnorn. Father had to close down his shop. What little savings we have is not enough to secure a new home elsewhere. We are truly stuck here.

I watch as my father and mother argue over my safety and His Grace's social standing. He's much too powerful to refuse. His wealth, his status, his relations with the king. Retaliation for rejecting him will be swift and unforgiving. If we thought Kilnorn cruel, then His Grace will be downright brutal.

My eyebrows pinch together as my teeth catch my lower lip. If he means to have me, if rejection means being unable to survive, then our best option is reaching for the title Duchess of Kilnorn. Lydia's words fill my head. *Love will not warm your house or put food on your table.* If she were here, she would tell me to acquire an engagement, to appease him if it means ten thousand rysar a year. Otherwise, he will force our hand and I will reap none of the benefits of his title.

I look around our small abode, at the single bed Mother and I share, at the straw mat Father sleeps on, at the worn and wobbled table, at the layer of dirt upon our floor. If I were to become duchess, Father and Mother could come live with me. Father wouldn't need his business. He could comfortably retire. If I were to become the duchess, people would no longer openly scorn me. My status would strike fear in their hearts. I could punish them for their cruelness. They'd have to think twice before acting out against me. My family would go from social outcasts to the most powerful people in town.

His Grace Gryphon Pike is a terrifying man. But he may be our only salvation.

"Father, I require money for a new dress," I suddenly announce as I stand to my feet.

Their argument immediately stops as they both turn to face me. Father looks as though a vein is about to burst. Even Mother appears put off by my demand. Still, I do not yield. My head remains high as I wait for his reply.

"Have you gone *mad?*" he asks. "I cannot squalor away what little fortune we have simply because you would like a new dress."

My shoulders pull back as my fingers curl into fists. Determination lines my face. I will not yield.

"I will need it to attend His Grace's ball."

Dawning shines on my mother's face as she realizes my true goal. Father is not so quick to understand. Of course, why would he? As a man he never had to consider such things. I clear my throat, some of my determination deflating but my voice is firm.

"It is my intention to acquire an engagement from His Grace and to do so, I must attend his ball."

Chapter Seven

Gryphon

- present day -

Lydia SCOWLS AT the empty ballroom before her, her hands clamped tightly below her bosom. I can't help but study the tension holding her in a vise grip, her mouth clamped shut as her brown gaze burns with the hatred of the world. I barely know her, yet there is no denying what a formidable woman she is.

"You are to tell me, Your Grace, that *none* of my shipments have arrived?" she asks, tone clipped and breath tight.

"Indeed," I answer simply and offer nothing else.

"We are scheduled to hold the ball within two weeks and you have received *none* of the orders I've placed?" she questions again and my temples pulse in agitation.

"Yes," I answer gruffly.

"Your Grace," Lydia begins calmly but I do not miss the fire within her tone. "I offered my services to *help* plan the ball. I am not the Duchess of Kilnorn. It is not my—"

A low, threatening growl echoes within the ballroom, bouncing a little too clearly off the walls. If she thinks it too similar to a living, breathing animal, her face does not show it. Instead, she scowls more deeply but in my direction.

"Your Grace," she snaps, all niceties gone from her voice. "If it is your intent to court Miss Elvira, then I suggest you take this ball more seriously."

The words cut through me, a reminder of the life I've condemned myself to. I'm more beast than man. I shouldn't be hosting parties, but my attempts of *courting* Elvira were met with much resistance. It was unwise to call upon her so soon after my arrival, yet I couldn't stay away. She calls to me, a moth flying towards its death if only to get a mere glimpse of the beautiful flame.

A huff of indignant breath passes through my nose. "I take this ball as seriously as I take this town."

A sharp laugh tumbles out of Lydia, her eyes rolling skyward at my words. She thinks I jest, but she knows so little of the choices I made to own Kilnorn, of the sacrifices I made all so that Elvira will be *mine*.

Her eyes slide to mine, a coy smile upon her lips. "Your Grace, Kilnorn is a pit one must stop at on their way to Hell."

"But it is the pit where Elvira resides."

Her brown eyes flash, her shoulders turning towards me as a calculating look overtakes her fierce features. Strange that she reminds me so much of Silas in this moment. A prickling razes the back of my neck as she studies me, her eyes seeing things I do not wish to give away.

My lips pull back in a snarl, my body tensing under a threat it doesn't fully understand.

"You seemed rather... intent on your first day here, Your Grace," Lydia speaks and I do not miss the subtle step she takes *away* from me. "As if you were seeking someone very specific. How could that be when you've never stepped foot in Kilnorn?"

My shoulders scrunch, my fingers curling to my palms. I will not have anyone interfering with what is *mine*. If I must remove Lydia to protect what belongs to me, I will not hesitate.

She must sense the underlying danger for she takes another subtle step away.

"I've heard of men in Edlercross who like to collect women like prized dolls," she continues.

Her eyes remain guarded, her grip loosening as she creates more distance between us. She intends to provoke. To see how I shall react to her inquiries, to see the hidden answers I give away without knowing. She desires to uncover the *real* truth. The sharpness of her eyes tells me she will not stop until she has it all.

A growl rumbles low and deep. She is too much like Silas. She'll soon have a collar tightly wound around my neck if I am not careful enough.

"I've never fancied dolls, Miss Cyprian. I am not like the men in the city."

"No," she hums her agreement, eyes never wavering from me. "You are not. Tell me, how did you come upon your title? Were you a childhood friend of the king?"

I cannot help it. My body steps to her on instinct. Her eyes widen for the briefest of seconds before she schools her expression. She takes a step back, not allowing me the pleasure of bearing down on her any more than I already do.

"Silas and I grew close a year ago," I tell her because if I do not tell her, she will pry where she shouldn't.

If she were not someone so important to Elvira, if I knew Elvira would not forsake me in her grief of losing her, I'd rip Lydia's head off in a heartbeat. Yet despite my short stay within Kilnorn, even I have gathered how closely the two are.

They're social pariahs in a wayward town. One touched by a witch, the other by misfortune. Their other friend, a pious woman, nothing more than a snake in wait. She is no threat of mine but Lydia Cyprian with eyes too similar to Silas is a threat I cannot afford to have. If I cannot kill her then I must offer short truths.

Her brows pinch together, mind calculating information I have not given. Bloodlust thrums within my veins, the desire to kill this threat before me salivating my mouth. My bones crack and grind against each other, the wolf begging to be released. Kill. Kill. KILL!

She must sense the danger for she finally casts her gaze from me, the trinkets within her braids chiming from the movement.

"I expect you to contact the vendors *today*, Your Grace. Find my orders or this ball will be for naught."

ELVIRA HUMS A low tune, her rifle held loosely within her hands as her feet crunch against dead leaves. Her muted clothes blend well into her surroundings as she checks the traps within the forest around her house. She's unaware of the beast that lurks within the woods hunting her.

She stops, her feet pushing aside rotting leaves as she inspects yet another empty trap. Fiery orange hair is braided down her back, little wisps blowing gently in the wind. A frown pulls on her lips and a rumble vibrates through me. Soon those lips will be doing much more.

Her gaze snaps towards mine, confusion lacing her expression as she searches. I crouch lower into the brush and hold still. Time stretches between us as she refuses to look away. A chuckle bubbles its way up from my chest. Her instincts must know danger is near.

Much to my amazement, she raises her rifle in my direction. The action is well practiced and done with such ease. An odd trait for women but not one for a *witch*. How fitting that the witch of Kilnorn has tamed the beast.

Curiosity gets the better of me and I venture out towards her. Her pale blue eyes widen as she immediately spots me. How could she not? My size is unnatural, more beast than wolf.

Her finger curls around the trigger of the gun, pupils dilated as she forces her breath to remain calm. Will she shoot me? I'd let her if she so desires it. Her gaze darts to my wrist for the briefest of moments, realization dawning on her as she spots the remnants of my scar poking through overgrown fur.

"Your wound has healed well," she states, voice trembling despite her best attempts.

Soon. Soon it will tremble with desire.

A low growl echoes within the forest at the thought. She will be *mine*. Even if the ball is a disaster, I *will* have Elvira.

I sit twenty feet from her, head cocking to the side as I stare at her. She frowns, the rifle sitting loosely in her grip as the barrel aims towards the ground. She relaxes, the tension dispelling from her shoulders, but her frown deepens.

"Your eyes," she says, brow furrowing.

Yes, she noted my eyes the first time we met. She stared death in the face and did not see the beast bearing down on her but the human that lurked within. The first ever to notice such a thing.

"Well," she breathes out. "If we're to be meeting like this I shall give you a name. Does Mr. Pike suit you?"

She dares to use my surname? A gruff bark of laughter tumbles out my maw. Her eyes narrow in suspicion as if she *knows* I am Gryphon Pike, Duke of Kilnorn stalking her in the woods to acquire what is mine.

"I trust that it does," she says simply. Her gaze turns to the trap near her feet, then back to me. "Have you been eating the game in the area? All my traps are empty. If you are to continue to hunt this territory then I must implore you to share your earnings."

A snort of sorts exhales through my nose. It's cute she deems it necessary to negotiate with the beast. Yet the striking reality is that in this moment, I realize I wouldn't have any other woman who *wouldn't*.

Yes, I was right in owning this town to make her mine.

Her lips press into a thin line, her hands curling a bit tighter around her gun. "I trust you'll leave a payment by sundown, Mr. Pike. I would detest to take your fur but I will. If the next time I see you is without game, your fur will be mine."

As it should be.

For good measure, she lets loose a shot. It burrows into the ground inches from my paw. An excellent shot. Rather unbecoming of a woman and yet it only makes me desire her more.

I rise to my feet. She remains unmoving, determined not to show fear in front of the unnatural wolf. I offer a bow, nose brushing against the dirt. A slight quirk of her lips, a glimpse of a smile, has finally been offered to me. It is more alluring than I could have anticipated.

With a shake of my fur, I leave to go fetch the game she rightfully demands as payment. Hours later, after dropping off several medium and small sized game for her, I return back to the Lockwood Estate. Blood stains my chin, neck, and chest as I walk naked through the foyer.

"I see the beast is alive and well. I must admit, I feared Kilnorn would bore the wolf to death."

Silas Ambrose stands near the parlor entrance, a glass of whiskey within his hand. He's dressed ornately, golden embroidery clashing against navy cloth. An unusual style not worn by any of the previous royals. Perhaps he intends to shift the style worn among his court in a subtle move of proving his power to those unhappy with his ascension. Either way, I do not care. It doesn't involve me.

My eyes narrow in suspicion, anger lancing down to my fingertips as a snarl escapes my mouth. His visit is unannounced. There could only be one reason the king would venture so far away from the capital. He requires someone's untimely death.

"No bow or greeting?" Silas inquires, a gentle *tsk* floating in the air, but the amusement in his eyes does not match his words. "I could have you killed for that."

"I offer no arguments," I reply simply and he cackles, head falling back and exposing that supple neck.

My teeth ache to sink in, to rip flesh from bone, to have blood splatter across my maw and on the too pristine marble floor. Instead, I walk towards the stairs. I'm in need of a bath.

Silas silently watches me as I walk past him and up the steps. He does not follow. He does not say anything. He merely watches me disappear from his sight. I do not know how much time passes but I make no effort to quicken my pace. I enjoy a long, hot bath, wiping all evidence of blood from me. My thoughts linger to a supple mouth, to fiery orange hair, to fierce pale blue eyes. I'm so close to having her, to owning her fully, I can practically taste her on my mouth.

I eye the glass bottles adorning the edge of the bath, scents and oils fit for the Duke of Kilnorn. Perhaps Elvira desires a man with a rich smell but I cannot bring myself to use them. The scents greatly irritate my nose, drowning all ability to smell anything at all. She will simply have to learn to enjoy my natural scent. But remnants of rosemary fill my memory and against my better judgment, I dabble eucalyptus oil behind my ears as I vacate the tub.

Eventually, I find my way back down to the parlor. Silas lounges near the fire, his whiskey glass forgotten as he reads one of the many books left behind from the old duke. He looks so little like his father. So much so, I briefly question his relation. Perhaps the queen had an affair. Honestly, it would explain why Silas is so different from the late king and prince.

"Enjoy your bath?" he inquires, interrupting my thoughts.

"Who do you need killed?" I ask, cutting straight to the chase.

I've no need for pleasantries with him.

"No one at the moment," Silas answers. "I'm here to attend the ball Miss Cyprian asked I participate in. Normally, I wouldn't bother with a waste of a town but I had to check in on my dearest wolf. See how he's faring. You're doing better than I imagined but I see there's no *Duchess* of Kilnorn. I'm surprised. I thought for sure a poor young woman would be locked up in one of these many rooms, but alas. They remain empty."

"Spying on me, I see," I reply gruffly.

It's to be expected. Neither of us has trust in the other. I am not surprised to find out he would go snooping when no one greeted him upon his arrival. Then there's the fact that I know all of his passages within the castle. He must feel at a disadvantage. The snooping about in the Lockwood Estate must make him feel on even ground.

News of his invitation is something Miss Cyprian failed to gain my approval for. With that sharp mind of hers, I can only surmise it was done so willingly. She's not one to casually forget an invitation to the king, after all. No matter. Those flowers she believes will go perfectly in the ballroom will be lost in transit. It's the petty things that matter when dealing with people like Lydia and Silas.

Quietly, I cross the parlor to a grand chair across from Silas. He says nothing, merely closes the book and tosses it on the end table.

"You'll have to introduce me to Miss Cyprian. I must meet the person so bold as to invite the king without the duke's consent or awareness. She must be one Hell of a woman."

A snort is all I offer him. Having her removed from Elvira's side would do me favors. If he desires to kill her, then who am I to object? I wish to share Elvira with no one and Lydia is not someone I can so easily remove myself. If the king were to do it, then he'd bear the title of monster, not I. Better yet, Elvira will come to *me* for comfort. Yes. Introducing Silas and Lydia is a great idea. Fantastic even.

"It will be my pleasure, Silas."

I don't miss the way his temple ticks at my lack of title or respect. But there are no witnesses here and I will not falsify respect where there is none.

"Tomorrow," I say, a smirk spreading across my lips. "I shall make your acquaintances tomorrow."

And I will be that much closer to owning Elvira.

Chapter Eight

Elvira
- present day -

"His grace could not be any less prepared for the ball," Lydia grumbles as we enjoy our afternoon tea within the café.

She wears a lavender surcoat with a cream underdress, the pattern of the underdress remarkably beautiful and awe inspiring. Surely it would have been better suited for the ball than an afternoon tea with me. I openly gaped upon her arrival and, much to my chagrin, Lydia rightfully laughed in my face.

"Is it really that bad?" I ask before bringing the teacup to my lips.

"None of my shipments have arrived and he's to host the ball in seven days. He'll become the joke of Kilnorn. No one will respect him or his status."

"Perhaps he does not care," I offer, my thoughts trailing to the strange conversation we had the other day.

God wants no love of mine. A man who desires approval of others would never so boldly declare such animosity towards the powers that be. It was no less than blasphemy. He also does not speak kindly about the king. It's clear to me he cares so little about what others think about him. He's proven that even more so with his interest in me. He didn't even flounder when Father asked him about me casting him under a witch's spell.

"Then he should not be in possession of such a position. It is *wasted* on him," she practically hisses.

"Lydia," I chide, eyes glancing around the area.

If anyone were to hear her speaking about the duke in such a way, there would be repercussions I'm not sure she or her family could afford.

"You have my sympathies, Elvira," she sighs out, eyes rolling skyward as she ignores my attempts of dispelling the conversation at hand. "I cannot fathom a lifetime of his uselessness. Though I suppose Duchess would garner much more respect than Miss with the vendors. Maybe then the orders would be here."

"I don't understand why you offered to help plan his ball if it would grieve you so," I say. "Going on appearances alone, he didn't seem coordinated."

If I cannot dispel the conversation, then I shall join in. It's not like my family has anything more to lose either.

My comment earns a laugh from her and pride swells beneath my breast. Lydia has a peculiar sense of humor. It's not easy to make her laugh and she has no issue with letting you know whenever you fall flat. Each laugh I earn of hers is a treasured memory I cherish.

"I am under the notion he has more important matters on his mind," she hums into her teacup.

My eyebrow arches upon that sentiment. She must know something I do not. She has spent a great deal of time with His Grace. With that sharp mind and intellect of hers, she most certainly has learned of something.

"What has him so preoccupied?" I inquire.

She lightly shakes her head, lips pulling up towards the corner of her mouth. She *does* know something and she's not telling me! My eyes narrow, my lips pushing together to hide the smile daring to break free.

"Lydia Cyprian, I *must* implore you to share what you know," I state in a low voice as I lean over the small table between us.

Her smirk deepens as she shakes her head more fervently. The bell chimes as the door swings open. Out of habit, I turn to see who enters.

Annalise.

Her eyes widen briefly as she catches sight of me before she glances away, heading straight to enjoy tea with Mira. If Lydia senses the tension between Annalise and I, she does not touch upon it. She remains mute though the amusement has now gone from her face.

I haven't spoken to Annalise since our last conversation. I've thought about mending the rift between us but then that would be admitting a wrongdoing I never committed. If we are to move forward in our friendship, she must apologize. Sincerely.

My heart breaks at the notion our long standing friendship might possibly have come to an end, but I cannot overlook the horrid things she said about Lydia. And what must she say about me when I'm not within range? It's foolish I didn't understand it sooner. It's no wonder Lydia never warmed to Annalise. She must have known the moment she met Annalise. And I was the fool, blinded by something so naïve and simple as having two friends instead of one.

"Lydia," I hesitantly speak her name, drawing her attention away from Annalise. "I have not been a good friend to you."

Her eyebrow arches, the teacup pausing at her lips as she regards me with an indifferent stare.

"I do not expect absolution but I now realize I wrongfully regarded her as a friend towards you. Of course I was not blind to your friction, but I didn't see it for what it was. I'm sorry."

She sighs, her eyes sliding shut as her shoulders sink. "The world we live in, Elvira, hates us from the moment we are born. You will be burned at the stake while I will be drowned in the river. We're forced to tolerate what no sane man or woman ever would. While I cannot say I that dislike the sentiment of your acknowledgement and apology..."

Her eyes open, the rich dark brown of them shining with fierce determination. "As much as it grieves me to say this, Annalise is a resource for people like us. The town adores her. They do not scorn her for associating with the witch and the negro. For they believe she is doing God's work. If we were to lose her favor..."

The harsh truth slaps me hard across the face. As much as Annalise was using us, Lydia was using Annalise. One used for vanity and the other used for survival. Yet I was shamefully unaware of it all. How naïve can I truly be?

The bell chimes again as the door to the café swings open. My eyes drift towards the entrance, my mind a muddled mess, and I spot Duke Gryphon Pike as he steps through the threshold. He's not alone. A gentleman steps in behind him dressed so beautifully it dispels any thoughts I have.

Lydia shifts in her seat, fluffing the hanging sleeve of her surcoat. The heavy steps of the duke's boots thud against the wooden floor. I can only surmise he is headed straight towards us.

It comes as no surprise when he stops beside my seat, a gruff clearing of his throat as he threads his hands through his disheveled hair. The clothes may be made of the finest cloth but they do nothing for him. He appears as wild and feral as that unnatural wolf. Yet despite it all, I am still steadfast to secure a proposal from him. If only to protect my family from further poverty and disdain of the people in Kilnorn.

"Your Grace, how lovely to see you," I say, voice a little too saccharine for my liking.

Lydia's eyes flash, a knowingness dawning on her as a slow smile spreads across her lips. Her approval means more than it should. There is no judgment within her gaze. Only understanding. Understanding of the need for survival and what one must do to accomplish it.

"Likewise," he offers me his brute reply before turning to Lydia. "Miss Cyprian it would appear your unapproved guest as arrived. He has requested your presence."

Lydia coyly stands to her feet, eyes locked onto the handsome friend. Her hand drapes against her chest as she offers him a light bow. "It is my pleasure to make your acquaintance... sir."

He chuckles, airy and light, eyes alight with mirth. "Trust me, Miss Cyprian, the pleasure is all mine. Imagine my delight at learning Gryphon was unaware of my invitation. I must say, arriving at his house unannounced is the best gift I've ever been given. So thank you, Miss Cyprian, for coordinating that."

"I assure you that was not my intent," she says.

He laughs, a shake of his head as he steps towards her. "Come. Let us chat quietly over there."

"Of course," she says, a slight bow to her head before she walks over to an empty table towards the back of the café.

The duke plops down in her chair, the legs squeaking against the floor as it bears the full weight of him. His golden eyes watch the two of them settle at their table, a frown pulling at his lips and I cannot help the flash of wolf flitting through my mind. Odd he resembles the wolf so much. Odd the wolf reminds me so much of the duke. Yet even more peculiar was the game left upon the stoop of our home after my chat with the wolf. I did not know how to explain it to my parents.

"I fear Miss Cyprian has bitten off more than she can chew," the duke states, eyes sliding back to mine as he offers a tilted smile.

"Why do you look so pleased about it?" I cannot help but ask.

"She invited a guest without my approval. She will get nothing less than she deserves for bringing him here. He is not known for his kindness. I can only discern how he'll deal with her knowing he's nothing more than a pawn."

"But he had been so kind to her just now."

The duke huffs out a laugh. "He's a patient man. One used to wearing many masks."

My eyebrow arches, skin pimples flaring across my arms at a threat I do not fully understand.

"Then you must protect her," I insist. At the downturn of his lips, I add as affectionately as I can, "It would greatly please me."

His eyes flash wild. Not a moment later, he leans across the table, calloused hand stopping mere millimeters from mine. Piercing rich, amber eyes hold my gaze. My heart stops beating, my lungs stall, and my lips part as the intensity of Duke Gryphon Pike bears down upon me.

"And what shall I receive in return, Miss Noire?" he asks in a low rumble, his pinky finger ghosting against my index one.

Heat flares to my cheeks and I can no longer hold the intensity of his gaze. He looks as though he wishes to devour me. My heart thunders against my chest and I wonder if it's truly possible if my heart could break free from its cage.

My teeth catch on my lower lip. His fingers dig into the tabletop and my eyes flit up to his face. His pupils have dilated, his eyes glued to my mouth as the table digs into his body. He nearly consumes the small furniture in an effort to get closer to me.

I may not understand his fixation on me, but I understand the *power* of fixation. My eyes glance over at Lydia for the briefest of moments. She's heavily engaged with the mystery man. She would not hesitate to use any skill at her disposal if it meant getting what she required. She goes through life filling any role necessary as a means to an end. Something I never truly understood before today.

Inhaling deeply, my attention turns back to the duke. I offer a small smile, my gaze holding his. I cannot settle the rapid beating of my heart or the butterflies swarming my stomach, but I push through the fear. I can do this. I will not make myself a fool.

"It would greatly please me... Gryphon."

A growl emits from him, his eyes flaring to life as he nearly lunges across the table at me. I instinctively jolt in surprise and if he feels any ounce of shame for his behavior, he does not show it.

"Elvira," he growls my name and a foreign heat ignites down in my core. Such an intoxicating sound in the most sinful of ways. "Do not play games you cannot win."

Does he see through me so easily? He couldn't know my true intentions. Could he?

"Please," I beg, quickly folding to a more honest truth. Pretending to be someone I'm not is harder than I imagined. "She is my dearest friend. If you truly care for me as you so proclaim, you will treat her as though she were my blood and kin."

His eyebrow arches, eyes sliding beyond me as he nods his head in the direction behind me. "What of the blonde? Is she not a dear friend of yours?"

My eyes cast downward, ears burning at the implication of his words. Or perhaps not so much the implication but rather the discussion Lydia and I had right before his arrival. If this were any other day, my answer would simply be yes, she is a dear friend. But today... today I'm unsure. Can I forgive her? Or will I succumb to using her the way she and Lydia use one another?

"I..." the words die on my lips and his eyebrows crease.

Something in him shifts as he sits back in his chair, all demeanors of a feral animal gone save for his gruff appearance. He throws his arm carelessly over the back of his chair, no manners or airs of sophistication to be seen. He was never meant to be duke and yet, duke he is. I was never meant to be duchess and yet... he wants *me*.

"Regrettably there is nothing I can do. If he desires it, it will be done. That is the power he lords over us all. No kind words or just arguments will make a damn. He is the king, after all. What he wants done is done."

My mouth drops open, my eyes flitting over to where Lydia sits smiling so coyly at *King* Silas Ambrose the Third. She *invited* him? And without His Grace's knowing?

"My God," blows out of my mouth.

I knew she was a strong, determined, ambitious woman but I never understood how deeply it ran. To invite the king even *with* His Grace's consent is madness, yet she did it on her own and without fear.

A laugh of disbelief leaves my lips and just as I do, the king turns his head ever so slightly towards the side, offering me the profile of his face. He's smiling. No tension, no overlaying threat, no danger to be seen. He's smiling and he's smiling *at her*.

My heart skips a beat upon realizing if Lydia's plan works accordingly, she could be, at worst, the king's mistress and, at best, his *wife*. A mistress is not so shameful when it's the *king's* mistress. She will be showered with wealth, status, and respect but knowing Lydia, she will not settle for anything less than queen.

"I fear he has no idea whom he is up against," I state, nodding my head towards the two. "He seems rather transfixed, wouldn't you agree, Your Grace?"

His face scrunches in distaste. "So, it is Your Grace now that she requires no help of mine?"

I cannot help it. I cannot keep up the rouse of using him for the sake of my family's well—being. I cannot ignore this unpleasant knowingness between us that he only seems to have. I do not know him and yet, he is relentless in us being together.

"Your Grace, I do not *know* you. I do not understand why you sought me out upon your first day in Kilnorn. I do not know why you are so determined to make my acquaintance. I've had many men approach me for disgraceful reasons. Are *you* such a man? Do you intend to marry me or discard me after getting what you desire?"

He barks out a loud laugh, his head thrown back as he draws the attention of those within the café. I try not to shrink in my seat but when the *king* turns to look at us, I can't help it. Heat flushes my face, my neck, my ears. I must resemble a tomato.

I flinch as he slaps the table. He leans forward yet again, eyes gleaming as a crazed look befalls his face.

"Elvira Noire, I have no such intentions of discarding you. You are *mine* and none other shall have you."

A gasp but not my own. A chair scraping against the floor and a fluttering of cloth. I cannot break away from His Grace's intense stare but Mira's voice cuts through the deafening silence.

"Annalise," she calls after her, the bell chiming as the door closes behind them.

A quiet hum begins to fill the café once more as neither I nor His Grace says another word. He watches me, that crazed look slowly disappearing from his features. My mind races as I digest the words he's spoken. Dangerous words of a crazed man. Would I be forfeiting my life simply to salvage my father's business? Is it worth the danger of this man?

"I am property to be owned," I state, the words bitter but true.

I am the witch of Kilnorn. No man would ever love me. I should be grateful that one desires to *own* me. Especially one of such status and wealth. Still, the reality leaves ash upon my tongue and a pang within my heart.

"Property?" he asks, an arch of his eyebrow as he shakes his head. "You are not property for me to own. You are merely *mine*. Wolves mate for life, Elvira Noire. You've no other choice."

Ice runs through my veins. *Wolves mate for life*. Why would he use such a phrase? As he and I are not wolves, it matters not that they mate for life and yet... I cannot unsee him as the wolf I've stumbled upon twice. The eyes. The feral nature of their presence. The air about them. If he were to tell me in this moment they are one and the same, I would believe him without a doubt.

"Come, Pike," the king's voice cuts in, drawing our attention. "We must ensure this ball is the talk of the town for at least an entire year. Miss Cyprian's reputation is on the line here. I will not risk a single smear against her."

Lydia stands beside him, sure and proud, as she stares down at His Grace. Whatever punishment he thought she'd receive has been thwarted by her intellect and grace. She is a formidable foe and, with her expertise of how society is within the capital, she will surely run circles around the duke. He is unrefined and uncultured. He doesn't stand a chance against her.

Although, he doesn't need to be those things out here in Kilnorn. His wealth grants him enough status and power. There's no need for pleasantries or refinement. He is free to live how he desires and no one here would dare to question it for fear of retaliation. But Lydia aims higher and where I believe she intends to go she'll require that wit and grace more than ever. Vultures will await her if she is to achieve her goal.

A deep exhale blows from His Grace's mouth. He languidly stands, his movements stiff as he lifts his head to stare down at the king. No fear within his eyes. Only animosity.

"You wish to *help* Miss Cyprian?" he inquires, the tone not hiding any of his displeasure.

The king's smile deepens, a playful mirth dancing within his gaze. "I do. Come, come. We have much to prepare."

His Majesty's gaze turns to mine and he offers me the smallest head bow. I jolt out of my seat and straight into a rough curtsey. Mumblings of how strange I am float around the room. No one here knows the king is within our midst. King Silas's self—portrait hasn't made it this far out from the capital. We haven't had the opportunity to see what he actually looks like. To the people of Kilnorn, I'm the crazed witch curtseying an outsider.

The king seems unperturbed by my actions. Perhaps a little amused but it is short lived. His attention almost immediately returns to Lydia, his smile sharpening the slightest bit.

"It was my greatest pleasure making your acquaintance Miss Cyprian. I truly look forward to more interactions."

"As do I."

She offers him no curtsey. Instead, she bows her head in the same manner he showed me. A quick, brief action, lips pulling at the corner of her mouth. He chuckles as he turns to His Grace. A harsh slap on his shoulder before the king tugs the duke towards the door.

"We have much to discuss, Pike," is the last thing I hear before the two disappear out of the door.

Immediately, I whirl around, hand clamping around Lydia's wrist before I drag her towards the corner where she sat with the king.

"Lydia I cannot believe you would be so reckless," I whisper lowly as my eyes flit about the room.

I know they do not know he was the king, yet I still worry of eavesdropping ears. What would they say? How would they react?

Thankfully, everyone seems to be ignoring us as we have our private conversation towards the back of the café. No one cares about what the outcasts have to gossip about.

"His Grace made it quite clear he only has eyes for you," Lydia answers as she plucks her wrist from my grip. Her rich brown eyes hold my gaze as she steadily speaks, not an ounce of worry or fear within her voice. "With Duchess of Kilnorn belonging to you, I required another solution. Her Majesty has a nice ring to it, doesn't it?"

"I cannot believe he let you off so lightly," I say with a shake of my head as I process the turn of events. "You didn't even inform His Grace of whom you invited."

Lydia waves her hand dismissively, the length of her hanging sleeve swaying from the action. "He would never have sanctioned it. He may weave a tale of close relations but it is clear His Grace and His Majesty share discontent with one another."

"Mm, I must agree. Which is why I find it so surprising His Majesty did not punish you."

"Punish me? My friend, he rejoiced at catching His Grace off guard. Men are such simple creatures to please, Elvira. Learn it, use it, and *flourish*."

She doesn't wait for me to respond. Instead, she quickly bids me farewell before walking out to the street and disappearing within the dense fog over Kilnorn.

Chapter Nine

Gryphon
- present day –

"KILNORN IS MINE," I declare as Silas and I make our back to the Lockwood Estate.

"What is the average tax collection?" he asks effortlessly, hair slightly jostling from the rough carriage ride. His eyes slide to mine, no amusement or joy upon his face. "Oh, forgive me. That's not something you would know as you are simply *acting* like a duke."

"I *am* the Duke of Kilnorn—"

"Then behave like it," Silas snaps at me. "I did not grant you dukedom for you to squander it on some witch's cunt."

I move swiftly, hand wrapping tightly around his neck as the weight of my full body bears down on him. His eyes widen, fear making them glossy as he struggles against my grip. I've cut off his ability to speak and the guards surrounding the carriage remain unaware of what transpires within.

"Speak ill of her one more time," I snarl as my fingers dig into his neck.

He flails against me, fist slamming into my shoulder. The reality must be settling in now. If I do not unhand him, he *will* suffocate to death. The thought makes me smile.

I lean forward, my hand still tightly around his throat as I speak. "Kilnorn is *mine*. Speak ill of her once more and that pretty little crown of yours will be six feet underground."

I hold him for a moment longer to solidify my words before releasing my grip. He gasps for air, abruptly shifting as far away from me as possible as he holds his neck. I sit back in my seat, my gaze drifting out the window.

"You will be killed for that," Silas states.

"No man truly has power, Silas," I lazily reply. My eyes slip to his, a grimness befalling my features as I speak. "You sanction my death and the country will know what you did."

His temples pulse. He knows it shouldn't matter if the country knows what he did. He is the king now. He won't be tried for murder even though he had only been a prince when he killed his father and brother. Still, the people will *know* what he did. The people will speak. They will whisper amongst the street and in the corridors about the king who allied himself with the Devil. Silas will never know peace. And if his luck were to truly turn for the worst, the Church would use its influence to sanction his death.

His secret can never be known. He knows that. He is as much in this mess as I am. He cannot kill me unless he so desires to die himself.

Silas lets loose a heavy breath, hand running through his hair. "My greed will be my death," he mutters to himself.

Good. At least he's aware.

The rest of the carriage ride is in silence. And if my lack of respect shows a bit more, it is not done so with intent.

SHE IS A vision in emerald green, hair perfectly styled, cheeks freckled and rosy as she enters the room. Heat thrums through my veins, my throat thick as I swallow. Her pale eyes cast about the room and my heart races in anticipation. When her gaze catches mine, she stops and so does my heart.

She speaks softly to the man beside her – her father I quickly realize. His lips pull downward but he nods his head. She offers him a small smile. Jealously lances through me, a growl rumbling within my chest. That smile is mine. Not his.

I nearly lunge across the room to tear his throat out, father be damned, but she steps towards me. A sharp inhale passes through my lips as she crosses the room, avoiding bodies as best she can. They seem more than happy to step out of her way, her reputation of witch preceding her. Good. No one should touch her but me.

When she stops beside me, rosemary and lavender tickle my nose. My nostrils flare as I stare down at her. She does not lift her head, instead staring up at me through her lashes. A seductress's move. My lips peel back in a predatory smile. She knows what she's doing and she does it so well.

"Miss Noire, I trust the ball is to your liking."

"It is," she speaks confidently, a slight tremor to her voice.

Soon. Very soon that tremor will be because of me.

I cannot help it. My body is its own and I do nothing to stop it. My hand is upon her waist, pulling her flush against my side. She inhales sharply, a protest upon her lips but it dies in her mouth as I lower my head to hers.

"That greatly pleases me, Miss Noire. As this party is entirely for you."

Others around us gape and whisper, their societal rules forbidding a man to touch a woman in such a way should they not be married. Rules be damned. This town is mine. I will do damn well whatever I desire and I shall touch what is *mine*.

"And how might you treat me should I say the ball is lacking?" she inquires, no movements to push away but the tenseness in her body tells me a story.

She is unfamiliar with being handled in such a way. Good. Though her pleasure is her own, the idea of her being comfortable in such an embrace boils my blood.

"If you so desire it, I will kick everyone out," I say, eyes capturing hers as I hold my face inches from her own. I dare to close the distance between us but know no good will come of it. It might very well scare her off. I must practice self—control. "If there was something specific you wished was in attendance, I would retrieve it. Whatever it is, you shall have it."

Her eyebrows furrow, confusion warping her face as she studies me. The seductress act disappears in an instance. As enjoyable as it was, the true her is even better. The one where she cannot hide her thoughts, the one where those thoughts so easily become words, the one where consequences be damned she will do as she pleases.

The true version of her is so much better than all the other versions she pretends to be.

"What is it that has you so bewitched?"

A low hum rumbles through my chest. A fair question. One I'm not sure she'll understand or enjoy the answer to, but I will hide no truths from her. The words spill from me with ease.

"A beast is a terrifying thing, Miss Noire. It's unnatural size, it's thirst for bloodlust, and no known predators of its own. So few people would be compelled to release it from a bear trap. And yet..."

Her eyes widen but I cannot discern if it is fear or understanding. Perhaps it is both.

"That day in the cold blizzard when you stumbled upon me, gun in hand... you were the most beautiful thing I'd ever seen. That day you released me," I say, voice dropping as my lips graze her ear, "you became *mine*."

"How?" she asks, body tugging against my hold for the first time since I grabbed her.

I allow her only an inch as I stand to my full height, my eyes bearing down at her as I read every reaction. She must know my truth if she is to ever truly be mine. I cannot have her fearing me, fearing what I become. She must know the shadows lurking within the closet. We will be stronger that way. A united pair. Mother was Father's strongest ally up until the day she died. She held his secret dear to her heart even years after his death. She went to her grave protecting him and the love they shared. Elvira and I will share in that same love.

"I had to do what pleased you to make you mine," I answer her. "And what is more tempting than the title Duchess of Kilnorn? I took this town *for you*."

She shakes her head, eyebrows deeply furrowed as she stares down at our feet. "No, no I do not care about that.

How is it that you shift shapes?" Her eyes snap up to mine, a frown pulling at her lips. "Do you come from the depths of Hell?"

My head throws back as loud, boisterous laughter fills the air. It startles a few near us but the lively chatter and music of the band drowns out most of it. She's tense, body itching to take another step away, but I do not let her. Now that she is within my arms, I will never let her go.

"There is no Hell among men or beast, Miss Noire," I tell her. "And there is no God either."

"That is not an answer, Your Grace," she firmly states, eyes narrowing as she silently demands the truth.

A strong, resilient woman. She will never relent. Her time as Kilnorn's witch has prepared her well to be my mate. The corner of my mouth quirks up. Perhaps there *is* a God for how else can I explain our first fated meeting? It is rather peculiar she was the one I met that day and no one else. I revel in it.

I carelessly look about the room, offering her a lazy shrug of my shoulders. "No one truly knows how we shift, Miss Noire. We tell ourselves we are descendants of wolves, that it is honorable to be part beast and man. But the truth is the people who knew the origins of our lineage have long since joined the earth. I've never cared enough to uncover the truth."

She's silent for a few moments, thoughts racing within her mind before she continues to speak.

"What will become of me?" she asks, the tremor back in her voice as she shakes within my grip.

"You? You are mine and no one else's. You are the Duchess of Kilnorn. There is no greater status you can have here—"

"And if I refuse, shall you lock me up within a cage? Or better yet, bury me in the ground?"

"You will *not* refuse," I snarl out, head dropping to be level with her own. "I took this town for you, Elvira Noire. Do not turn your nose up at me."

She lets out a huff of an indignant laugh instead of reeling back in fear. Such a curious woman to be so afraid in one moment, yet bold in the next. Confusion blossoms upon my face, the anger deflating from within as she offers me no kind words.

"Men and their egos are all the same no matter how *beastly* they are."

Fire ignites within her pale blue eyes, her shoulders pulling back as she pushes her finger against my sternum. Her nail is sharp as it presses through the thin layer of cloth and she makes no attempts to soften the pressure.

"Did I ask you to take this town in my name? No. You did what you wanted for *you*. Very well. I shall appease you and give you what you so desire. A taste of me, hm? And once you have it, gone you will be."

I nearly laugh. She has no idea the depths I have gone to make her mine, the sacrifices I have made. I will not have her once and be on my way. I will have her over and over until one of us no longer exists within this world. She is my only cure in this life, the same my mother was for my father.

"You cannot get rid of me so easily."

"No, I should hope not. But the dalliances of men are too predictable. I cannot imagine they should be so different for you."

Without another word, she turns away from me and heads towards a darkened hallway. Like a wolf hunting a rabbit, I chase after her, ignoring all townsfolk desiring to stop me for a chat. They do not matter. It is only *her*.

I follow the scent of rosemary and lavender, the faint smell disappearing down an unlit corridor. Her steps echo against the walls but I catch no sight of her. The thrill of the chase quickens my heart, my eyes dilating, my bones aching to transform but I hold back. I will not catch her in my wolf form. No. She will be caught by human hands and devoured by a human mouth.

I disappear down a second hallway, the Lockwood Estate vast and confusing. She knows not where she runs and the thought delights me. How should I find her? Timid, chest heaving, a pink flush upon her freckled faced skin.

My groin tightens against the constraints of my pants, a heat coursing through me viciously unchecked. She doesn't know what game she plays. No cries for mercy from her will be answered. When I find her, I will consume her.

Chapter Ten

Elvira
- present day -

MY HEART POUNDS against my chest, excitement splitting a grin across my face. The wolf hunts me within his grounds. He *will* find me, yet it is not fear I feel. My body is alive, flushed with desire and determination. I will hide from him for as long as I can but he will find me and when he does...

I run up a set of stairs, my feet tripping over my long dress. It's too dark for me to see where I'm running, but I'm steadfast in my pace. Heavy footfalls echo down the hallway and I nearly scream at being caught, the smile growing as big as it can. He's going to catch me. I must run faster.

I dart inside a room, not sure what it is. It could be a library, a study, one of the many bedrooms. It doesn't matter. I will hide from His Grace for as long as I can.

Hands blindly feel around for any sort of contact. They brush against silk cloth, a chair, and a desk before meeting a wall. I walk the length of it before finding a secondary door. Will it be a closet or entrance to another room? Only one way to find out.

I throw open the door and close it as quietly as I can. My hands shoot out, anticipating a closet, but it's another room. I sprint across as fast as I can, heart pounding in my ears as I search for the door.

"Elvira," his low voice vibrates through me down to my core and my knees nearly buckle.

The wolf flashes through my mind, unnaturally large and strangely understanding. Now I know why. They are one and the same.

"I can *smell* you, Elvira," he states in that low, enticing voice. "Rosemary and lavender but I desire to smell the real you."

"Oh God," I breathe out, mortified at the thought that he might smell things I would want to keep hidden.

The door clatters against the wall as he throws it open, eliciting a scream from my mouth. He laughs, low and threatening, as he stalks into the room. I can barely make out his frame within the dark of the room. He hunches as he stalks, head tilting this way and that as he sniffs the air.

"You are here, Elvira. Your scent is heavy and thick in the air. You've excited the beast. Now you must pay."

My hands shake, my breathing clipped as fear mingles with excitement. I'm terrified to be caught. I cannot wait to be caught. The rush of emotions intoxicates me, muddling my mind as I try and try and try to locate a way out.

"Tsk, tsk, tsk. You've given yourself away."

He lunges not a second later and a shrill scream bursts out of me. Hands grab at me roughly before lips sear against mine. Calloused fingers dig into my hair while a sturdy, rough body presses me against the wall. His weight bears down on me, warm and heavy and more than everything I desired.

His mouth attacks my own, tongue diving inside as he yanks my head back. He kisses me as if he means to eat me. I can hardly keep up, a novice at such things, but that doesn't slow him down. His hands are everywhere, igniting me with every sinful touch.

Fingers grip at my dress, yanking the cloth upwards to expose the most private parts of my body. Hesitation and fear have me fighting against him. I provoked the beast, I knew this would be the end result, and yet that little voice... *You're not married. You're defiling yourself. He has nothing to lose while you have everything.*

Teeth sinking into my neck derail my thoughts. His tongue laps at the spot, soothing the gentle ache. A gasp tears from me, my body jolting as his fingers slide along my wet core. A low hum of approval floats into the room before he slips a calloused finger inside me. He glides in and out with ease, building an ache deep within me.

Our labored breaths mingle together. His body humps against me, the stiffness of him pressing into my waist. The crescendo builds, his finger and thumb bringing me towards a salvation that only the Devil could know.

A whimper escapes me, fingers clutching him so tightly as my hips move against him. How natural my body moves in an activity I've never participated in. I know so little of what I'm doing with another body involved, but my confidence is not swayed. It brings me comfort to know that even if *I* may not know what to do, my body inherently does. And judging by the way His Grace is behaving, he is more than pleased despite my inexperience.

The loosening of a belt breaks through our heavy breathing. I've barely a moment to prepare, his words almost lost in the drunken haze of our dalliance.

"This will hurt. Do your best to relax."

He hikes my leg up, hoisting it around his hips, before the head of him pushes against me. He's right. It does hurt. He is much too large for my first time. The wetness helps, but it does not prevent the pain. I grit my teeth as he pushes all the way in. He grunts his approval.

A moment later, he's moving against me. The pain starts to subside with each glide he takes. My body responds to the slam of his hips, an understanding I don't fully comprehend. I only know the sensation of it all. How desperately he holds me. How ferociously he attacks me. How animalistically he growls. Each huff of breath, each grunt of pleasure, each rough grab of me tells a story of his feral enjoyment. That is enough for me. No matter what happens after this, it was worth it for his reaction alone.

His Grace continues his ministrations, hand squeezing me beneath the neck as his lips find mine once more. His kisses are rough, desperate, and full of greed. *I drown in them.* No man has ever wanted me in such a way. I was nothing more than a story they could tell their friends. A romp with the witch of Kilnorn. But I am so much more to His Grace, even with how little we know one another. I feel it in the way he devours me.

The thought that he became the Duke of Kilnorn for me had originally terrified me. What would such a man do if the one he desires were to say no? But now I understand it. That all consuming desire. That carnal greed to have it all. If I simply want it, it will be mine. His Grace will make sure of it. An opportunity of a lifetime has fallen into my lap and I would be nothing short of a fool to pass it up. I *must* seize it.

There may not be love between us yet, but there is room for it to grow, to bloom brighter and more beautiful than all the love that came before us. And if not... at least the title Duchess of Kilnorn will offer me status and wealth. May Annalise find the true love she desires, but I understand it now. Lydia probably understood it when she was far younger. Love does not sustain you. It does not put a roof over your head or food within your stomach or clothes upon your body. Status and wealth do.

My hands grip his face as I pull him back. He resists but relents.

"If I want it, duchess is mine?"

"Yes," he grunts.

"If I want it, the Lockwood Estate is mine?"

"Yes."

"If I want it, your fur is mine?"

He growls as the wolf I know he is and his hips stutter against me. "Yes. It is all yours. You only need claim it."

I pull him back into a kiss, hips shifting against his movements. He stutters more until he's grunting a release, teeth sinking into my flesh. A yelp of pain bursts from me and he shifts his hand to cover my mouth. The post coitus release shakes through him as his fingers dig into my cheek and jaw. He is not a kind lover but I would not expect that from a wolf.

When his hand shifts away from my mouth, I speak. "I want it. Give me the title."

"You are mine."

"Then reflect it. We are to be the witch and the wolf. Kilnorn is not yours, but *ours*."

He smirks, crazed and large, as he runs a hand through his hair. "So be it."

Chapter Eleven

Gryphon

- present day -

"COME," I ORDER as I quickly shove myself back into my clothes.

She doesn't question it as she hastily flattens her surcoat, adjusting the hanging sleeves. Her hair is coming out of its style but she is blissfully unaware. My heart thumps rapidly within my chest, an unknown excitement buzzing down to my feet. I grab her hand, yanking her through the room and out into the hallway. She does not question me, wordlessly following me through the large estate.

We descend the stairs, our footsteps echoing loudly against the stone walls. She struggles to keep up with my quickened pace, my stride too large for hers. I attempt to slow down but it feels too unnatural, too small. I stumble and she giggles. A sound I never thought I would hear.

My blood burns with greed and need. Once is not enough. But after we're through, I'll have a lifetime of her.

We burst through the doorway and straight into the ballroom. The music is lively, the people are drunk, and the room is hot and sweaty. A successful event if I cared. But perhaps Elvira cares. Perhaps I must succumb to a lifetime of social events but if that is the price I must pay for Elvira, then so be it.

I spot him quickly within the crowd, his attention following Miss Cyprian as she dances with some man. She's as elegant and sharp as ever. A perfect match for Silas Ambrose the Third. The two could accomplish much. Good *and* bad.

I push our way through the crowd, never bothering with niceties. Elvira holds my hand steadily as she follows my lead. A few moments later, I step into his view, blocking his ability to stalk Miss Cyprian. His eyes flash angrily as they meet mine. I waste no time.

"Marry us," I order.

His eyes widen for the briefest of moments, a slight flush to his face that I now realize means he's had one too many to drink. So unlike Silas. If I did not need him in this exact moment, I would take advantage of his drunkenness in a more fruitful way.

"What? *Now?*" he blusters, hands gesturing a bit aggressively and spilling his wine.

"Yes, now."

Elvira places her hand around my bicep as she steps forward, a small smile on her lips. A growl passes through my mouth. She shouldn't be smiling at anyone.

"Your Majesty, it would be a great honor if you were to marry us now."

"I am not a priest—"

"You are the king, are you not?" I cut him off.

The redness upon his cheeks darkens, his eyes narrowing as his lips pull downward in an angry scowl.

"I *am* the king, which means I take no orders from anyone."

"Please, Your Majesty. It would mean so much to us."

He arches a brow. "Us? You truly wish to marry such a beastly man? Do you even know—"

"I do," she interrupts him. "And I am not afraid."

"Foolish woman," he mutters to himself, eyes drifting to the wine within his goblet. Then cutting suddenly back to us. "Very well then. But let it be known, Miss. I *own* him. He comes when *I* call. *That* is the price he paid to have *you.*"

She nods her head knowingly. "Then I shall help him in any way that I can."

Silas laughs boisterously, head falling back as his hand slaps his stomach. Her words of support burn me up in flames. I move without knowing, hands gripping the sides of her face as I kiss her deeply. Music plays in the background, laughter and conversation consume the room, but it is just me and her. She hesitates only for the briefest of moments, hands coming up to grip my elbows as she kisses me back. Rosemary and lavender drown me as her petal soft lips send me to a heaven I know doesn't exist.

I hear the footsteps but think nothing of it. Then suddenly, I'm yanked backwards before a fist is thrown towards my jaw. I dodge, my arm pulling back in preparation of sending a killing blow forward, but Elvira steps in the way.

"Father!"

"You've tarnished her! You've ruined us!"

"No, I saved you," falls out of my mouth as I stand to my full height. "The king has married us. She is now *Duchess* of Kilnorn and you will treat her with the respect that title is given."

He looks aghast, his eyes darting back and forth between Elvira and me.

"*Married?*" he asks.

"Yes, Father. The king has agreed—"

"It has already been decreed. I'll draw up papers tomorrow," Silas states before swiftly walking away, attention mostly drawn towards none other than Lydia Cyprian.

"You—you cannot marry him! You're not safe with him! I did not give my blessings!"

"You are not happy with your daughter's newfound status?" I inquire, already plotting his untimely death.

She'll have to forgive me but I cannot have anyone spoiling her impressions of me. She is mine and I will not let her go. No matter what.

"Father—"

I grab her hand, suddenly spinning her towards the band, and yank her away from him. He protests, eagerly following after us but I pay him no mind. I walk straight towards the band and they immediately stop playing. The emptiness it brings silences the rest of the room. All the lively chatter dies within moments of the music stopping.

"Let it be known that today henceforth, Miss Elvira Noire is now Mrs. Elvira Pike, Duchess of Kilnorn. If I hear of any unkind treatment towards my wife, you will be swiftly dealt with. Kilnorn is under my rule granted by King Silas Ambrose the Third. I act in his good graces. Be forewarned."

A moment of silence and then the room bursts into a frenzy. I turn on my toes, a glare upon my face as I bear down on her father.

"She is no longer your responsibility Mr. Noire. Do not act hastily."

He swallows, his throat bobbing as he holds my gaze before very boldly stepping forward. "You hurt my daughter and I will kill you."

A laugh tumbles out of my mouth. "I'd like to see you try."

Elvira slaps me roughly across the shoulder, the only place she has access to at the moment. Anger flares through me as I turn on her but it immediately dies as I stare into her pale blue eyes. Pale blue *angry* eyes. There's fire there and I know she won't hold back.

"Of that entire statement, the part you focus on is his threat? And not of hurting me? 'I'd like to see you try' and not 'I would never hurt her, you have nothing to worry about, Mr. Noire?'"

My lips part to speak but for the first time in my life I am speechless. It only angers her more, her eyes narrowing as her lips pull downward.

"You so much as harm me, Your Grace, and *I* will kill you," she spits out, her face flushing and I cannot help the fire igniting within my veins.

Yes. She is mine. The only one to knowingly stand against the beast without power, without money, without status. Only sheer willpower and stubbornness and a kindness I'm too undeserving of.

My arms pull her in tightly, elation humming through me at now having what belongs to me. Elvira Pike. Elvira *Pike.*

My cheek presses into hers, her small frame devoured by my much larger one.

"If I harm you," I say, the words truer than any other I've spoken before, "I will give myself over willingly, Your Grace."

She tilts her head back, a seductive smile upon her face. It nearly knocks me off my feet to be the recipient of such a smile. I worked hard, sacrificed much, did such ungodly things to claim what I own and now, staring into that face, into that coy smile, into those eyes that stare right back into mine... God help me, I am doomed.

"You may be the wolf, Gryphon Pike, but I own the bear traps."

My laugh is the only reply she requires. She's the perfect match to my brute and she's all mine.

Mine.

Acknowledgements

Thank you Alexia for sensitivity reading this novella. Your input is highly valued and I greatly appreciate our working relationship. I look forward to many more collaborations in the future!

Zoë, Mackenzie, and Kim. You three make an astounding alpha reader team. I'm so fortunate that 1. You're my friends (and family) first and 2. That you're all unhinged readers. No matter how crazy or hectic your lives are, you always make time for me and my creations.

Zoë thank you for always, always, always reading everything I send you no matter how raw and incomplete it is. You read the 1.5 chapters of this story back in 2023 and you, without fail, answer all my wild texts about my inconsistent writing and it just means the absolute world to me.

Mackenzie your day to day support helps me get through the even the grimmest days. And your feedback on The Wolf and His Prey was the confidence boost I needed during my postpartum depression. I really wasn't sure what the hell I was doing (still don't, but we'll figure it out haha) but your trust in me and in my decisions always helped lead me in what I felt was the right direction.

Kim you are truly the brain of many of my projects. Your unending support of letting me bounce ideas off you, work out plot holes, and challenge me in the world I'm creating is why my stories have such solid grounds. You've been there at the very start when I was writing reader-insert fanfiction. I'm incredibly luck you stuck with me through it all. Thanks girly pop.

Brianna having you as an older sister who I can turn to when things get too crazy, who believes in me and my dream as enthusiastically as I do, who lets me say "I hate this!" on Monday and "I love this!" on Tuesday without calling me out is a gift I don't think you'll truly ever understand. It saddens me you don't have an older sister like I do. Being your little sister has been such a joy and privilege. Thank you for all you do for me both openly and behind closed doors.

Mom and Dad thank you so much for all your love and support. I really hate how far away you live. I miss you more than you know. And I really appreciate your support in my endeavor. It means a lot to me. I love you.

My children. You're the reason why I'm working so hard to make this dream a reality. I want to be an inspiration to you. To know no matter how "old" you become, you can always change your path. It will require hard work, some really fucking hard days — days that will want to make you give up —, and a fantastic support team. We are nothing without our community. You two are my world and I hope that one day I can share with you the journey it took me to get to where I am today.

Tuan you may not be a reader and therefore don't read what I write, but you've never made this feel like a child's dream. You've never belittled my passion for writing or told me I'd never make it as an author one day and these things may seem like common sense stuff not to say to a person but you'd be surprised. You've always shared in every little win I've had, making them bigger than they seem, and I can't explain how grateful I am for that. Thank you for supporting me in this and helping me follow my dreams. I love you.

Meet the Author

Alessandra Vu is a stay-at-home parent of two. She started writing reader insert fanfiction when she was 16 years old and gradually shifted over into original stories. Her favorite genres to read and write are fantasy romance (romantasy), paranormal romance, and urban fantasy romance. Her favorite book series is *The Hidden Legacy* by Ilona Andrews and her favorite comfort series is *The Lunar Chronicles* by Marissa Meyer.

alessandrao3330

Want to learn more? Use the QR code to view Alessandra's website, socials, and more!

www.ingramcontent.com/pod-product-compliance
Lightning Source LLC
Chambersburg PA
CBHW031842170626
46807CB00004B/1588